SECTOR C
THE HUNTED

by Nina Soden

I0460629

This is a work of fiction. All of the characters,
organizations, businesses, and events portrayed in this
novel are either products of the author's imagination or are
used fictitiously.

SECTOR C – THE HUNTED. Copyright © 2015 by Nina
Soden.
All rights reserved.

ISBN: 978-0-9858853-4-2

The Hunted is the second book in the SECTOR C Series.

http://www.ninasoden.wordpress.com
Editor: Ula Manzo, Ph.D.
Beta Readers: Clara Tapaninen, Kevin Wade, and Jonas Lee
Cover Design by Nina Soden

This book may not be reproduced, transmitted, or stored in
whole or in part by any means, including graphic,
electronic, or mechanical, without the express written
consent of the author, except in the case of brief
quotations embodied in critical articles and reviews.

DEDICATION

For my loving family that never lets me give up. For my supportive husband who tells me every day how proud he is of me. For my beautiful children, whose creativity and joy make life a journey and an adventure. Lastly, for my readers—without you there would be no reason to write.

ACKNOWLEDGEMENTS

A special thank you to Ula Manzo, my patient, and excellent editor, for her attention to detail and amazing proofreading and editing skills.

1

"Murder!" His voice cut through the darkness.
Murder? What murder?

"What?" I jumped out of bed. "Who's there?"

Councilman Blake was sitting at the end of my bed, cloaked in the dark shadows. "Anything you want to tell me, Zelina?" He leaned into the light and his eyes burned with rage.

"I— No."

"Then you leave me no choice." One second Councilman Blake was sitting on the end of my bed, staring across the room at me with those dark black accusing eyes, and the next I was tied up, blindfolded, gagged, and being carried off into the night. I'm not even sure how it happened so fast. I struggled at first, but it got me nowhere. He was too strong, or I was too weak. Probably the latter, but it didn't really matter— either way, I wasn't getting away.

You need to know when to fight and when to plan. It was something Professor Gunner had said many times over the years. He knew that you can't

1

win every battle by just jumping in swinging. Planning and plotting have a lot to do with whether or not you make it out of a fight alive. I had a feeling this moment would be better served by planning my next move, not by kicking and screaming. Besides, Blake was a Councilman. Fighting him could jeopardize more than just how much sleep I got that night.

I listened as Britt followed behind, chastising him the whole way.

"Didn't I tell you this would happen? Didn't I warn you what she would do that—that she was a threat?"

"Did you?" He stopped and turned back to her so abruptly that I almost fell off his shoulder. "What was it you said? Yes, I remember, 'She isn't a threat. It was an accident, I'm sure of it.' Were those not your words, your exact words?"

Um, actually those were my words, I thought. However, there was no way I was speaking up and taking credit for them right now.

"No, I never—" Britt stopped herself. She couldn't defend herself without explaining what had happened. And she couldn't explain what had happened because she didn't know. She knew she had said those words—but she didn't know why, or what had made her do it. What she also didn't know was that he didn't need an explanation. He already knew. He was just waiting for the right time to expose me, at least that's what I thought at the time. "Father, I—"

After Selection Week, Britt had been assigned as my mentor, and I had been living in her apartment for these past few days. Since she was a nurse, and

Councilman Blake's biological daughter, it did make sense to have her put in charge of teaching me how to deal with my blood lust, and carrying out general babysitting duties. But she was also the one who had abducted me from my bed and injected me with the werelion virus during Selection Week. Let's just say she isn't the strongest advocate I could wish for right now.

"Watch what you say, Britt. You're walking a fine line. I wouldn't want you to get yourself into any more trouble than you are already in."

"But I—"

"You what? Do you think Zelina is the only one we've been watching?"

What? They're still watching me? When will this end? I had grown up in Sector C, and cameras were just a part of life. The Council watches over the sector students until after Selection Week for purposes of evaluating them. That's how it's always been. But to hear that they were still watching me, even after I had completed Selection Week—and with flying colors I might add—felt as if they were hoping I would fail—or do something that would make them turn on me. As if what I am, what they had made me into, is my fault and not theirs. I shouldn't be punished for their actions—their *choices*.

"No, sir, I...I meant no disrespect. I only wanted to explain—" She was backpedaling now, I could hear the pleas in her voice even without her begging words.

"You will have plenty of time to explain when we get to the Council offices."

3

Well, at least I know where we're going now.
However, it did seem like we were taking the extra-long route.

"Must I, father? Can't you just let me—?"

"Let you go? Is that what you were going to ask?"

"I—"

"I have been very patient with you over the years Britt. More patient than most would think appropriate. This time, you have gone too far. It is for the Council to determine your fate. I can no longer protect you."

"But—"

He turned and started walking again. At first I didn't think Britt had followed, but then I heard the shuffling of her feet on the road behind us.

I must have fallen asleep or passed out at some point, but I can't say that I remember it happening. What I do know is when I woke up I was no longer blindfolded. I was, however, tied to a chair in the middle of a windowless room that was not any of the Council offices I had seen so far. There was a sharp pain in my arm when I tried to move. When I looked down, I noticed that a needle, connected to an IV, had been fastened into the inside of my arm.

Instantly, I started to feel nauseous and dizzy. Needles have that effect on me—I can't explain it and I'm not proud of it.

Across the room I could see Councilman Remy, the Sector C Leader, standing between two groups of angry Sector Council members. The Vampire Council members—Blake, Serenity, and Ash—were standing to his right; the Lycanthrope

Council members—Cruz, Iris, Donovan, and Phoenix—were all standing to his left. It seems that even in their private meetings they can't seem to play nice.

They must not have noticed that I was awake because they were arguing among themselves. Everyone was talking over each other trying to be heard, but no one was listening. Then one voice rose above the others.

"Why are you even here—any of you? It was a vampire who was killed and a vampire who drained him!" Serenity walked across to Councilman Donovan and spat in his face. "This is a matter for the Vampire Council, not the Lycanthrope Council."

He just stared down his nose at her, shaking his head in disappointment. "We both know that she is more than just a vampire. The blood of a lycanthrope runs through her veins as well. Therefore, if she had anything to do with his death—"

"Murder," Serenity corrected him.

"Fine, if she had anything to do with his murder, if it was a murder, then we feel that the lycanthrope laws should apply equally. We feel that we should have a say in her punishment."

Punishment?

"There is no proof that the lycanthrope virus has even affected her."

"There is no proof that it hasn't," he corrected her.

They're both right, I thought, and suddenly I realized that Merick had been right too. I had been so caught up in what it meant to be a vampire that I really haven't given much thought to the fact that I had also been infected with two of the lycanthropy viruses. He had tried to tell me, tried to show me that the wolf and lion inside of me needed room too, but I hadn't really listened.

"Fine." Serenity turned to Council Leader Remy. "Don't look at this as a Council matter— vampire *or* lycanthrope. Look at it as a security matter."

"Explain," Remy said.

"It happened within the sector walls, did it not?"

"It did. What is your point?"

"Since it happened within the sector walls, and I am in charge of internal sector security, I believe it falls under my jurisdiction. Had it happened outside of the sector walls I would gladly hand over the responsibilities to Councilman Donovan." Even without seeing her face I could hear the sweet, syrupy smile that she must have been giving Donovan right then. "I think you'll agree, sir, that I should be—"

"Stand down, Councilman Serenity," Remy said.

With those four little words, I was sure he had wiped the smile and smug attitude right off her face. "But sir—"

"Now!" He took a deep breath before addressing the group. "We are all well aware of what the child is."

I'm not a child! I decided not to argue, though. I was already in enough trouble—besides, it wouldn't have done me any good.

"What she is capable of is still undetermined. We have all heard Britt's testimony, and although I have respected her opinion in the past, in this situation I do not agree with her recommendations. I also feel that she is no longer capable of maintaining an unbiased assessment of the situation." Serenity became restless, turned away, and leaned against the far wall. She was struggling not to argue her point again. "This is not the first murder we have covered up in Sector C and I am confident it will not be the last."

Serenity couldn't stop herself. "Sir, you can't possibly—"

"Stop right there." He spoke slowly, in a tone that was not to be argued with. "If you interrupt me one more time, I will have you removed from this meeting and banned from all future Council initiatives. If you continue this disrespectful behavior, Nurse Britt will not be the only one losing sector privileges tonight. Do I make myself clear?"

"Yes, sir." As she turned and took a seat in one of the empty chairs, I wondered what it meant that Britt would be losing her sector privileges.

Serenity had turned her back to the rest of the Council members, and I could see her face as she stared down at the ground. She was flushed with rage, and I couldn't help but tap into her emotions. I closed my eyes, and when I opened them I was there in her seat staring at the floor. I looked over at my own body, bound and gagged in the chair across the room. I could feel Serenity struggling to understand what was happening to her—inside of her—she didn't know it was me. She tried to speak, but I stopped her. She turned, and I could feel the panic welling up inside of her as she reached for Councilman Ash, who stood just to her left.

7

"Are you all right?" he asked, but something distracted him. He turned to me, to my tied up body, and for a second I thought he knew. "If we are finished squabbling among ourselves," he announced, "I believe the child is awake."

Oh no, he does know. He knows.

2

"Take your seats," Remy commanded. Everyone moved to follow his orders, robotically taking their places. Vampires to his left and lycanthropes to his right, they arranged themselves in a semi-circle across from where my body now sat tied to the chair, limp and lifeless.

I pulled myself out of Serenity's mind and slipped back into my own. I didn't open my eyes, not right away. Instead, I pretended to just be waking up. I tried to reach for my head and struggled against the ropes I already knew were there. "Watt? Wha mm a tid uup?" I mumbled through the gag. When I finally did open my eyes, I looked around the room, scanning their faces, "Whass appinin?" I coughed and almost choked on my own saliva. *OK, talking is out of the question.*

"What's happening? Are you kidding?" Councilman Serenity asked.

I shook my head, not wanting to choke again. When I met Councilman Blake's jet black eyes, he smiled. He actually smiled.

"Wonderful, you're awake. I'm so glad you've finally decided to join us. I was worried I'd have to resort to…less than desirable measures to wake you."

He smirked as if he would have enjoyed his *less than desirable measures*.

"Let the girl speak," Councilman Remy said, motioning to Blake.

Blake stood and took a step forward—a step closer to me. "I'm going to take the gag off now. Can I trust that you won't scream?"

I nodded and he took another step forward. I probably should have been afraid, but I wasn't. There was something about the way he walked—hesitant, almost timid—and the way he looked at me, as if maybe I was the real threat. This from the man who had come into my room in the middle of the night, bound and gagged me, and then carried me off over his shoulder. He circled behind me, and I could feel him tugging at the knot that had been digging into the back of my head. At last, the gag dropped to the floor and I gasped for a deep breath that I didn't really need.

As vampires get older, they develop the ability to go for extended periods of time without breathing. I think it has something to do with the reduced heartrate. Whatever it is, it develops over time. Now, when I say extended periods of time I mean fifteen to twenty minutes, even up to thirty for the oldest vampires. It helps with the creepy statue-like stillness they are so good at.

I haven't even been a vampire for a full two weeks, and I have already started noticing significant changes, advanced development, in myself—one of which is the ability to go for almost five minutes without air. During the time I had spent living in Britt's apartment—in her charge—I'm pretty sure she had also observed many of the changes I was going through. I hadn't actually talked to her about them though, or she to me, so I wasn't sure exactly what or how much she had noticed. I also couldn't be sure how much she had shared with the Council or her father.

I made the quick and conscious decision to hide this one little fact about myself right now, as I gasped for breath. I figured any advanced signs of vampirism would be interpreted as proof that the vampire virus was dominant in me and then maybe Remy actually would turn me over to Serenity. Although I wasn't a hundred percent sure what she would do to me, I did know I didn't want to find out.

"Is there anything you'd like to tell me—*us*?" Blake asked, as he walked back around to look me in the eye.

"I—no sir. I'm not sure what you're talking about."

"No, no of course you're not." He turned his back to me and approached Remy. "How would you like to proceed?"

"You may question her. If you cannot get her to speak freely, and quickly, we will rely on other methods to get answers," Remy replied.

"I can make her talk!" Serenity said.

Remy just shook his head. "I don't believe that threats will get this one to speak. Besides, we should give her the benefit of the doubt; she is still one of us."

"She isn't one of us, and I wouldn't *just* be threatening her." She was staring right at me, and I could feel her laser-like gaze burning through my skull. Serenity is beautiful—tall and slender, yet muscular, with short blond hair that perfectly outlines her exquisite face. Yet, despite her name, she is one of the least serene people I've ever met.

"What she *is*, is what *we* made her." Remy replied. "You ought not to forget that. The vampire inside her is the same as yours and mine! The wolf, the lion—they are no different than those of any other lycanthrope. We will treat her as a sector resident until we have proof of her guilt. Then and only then will we seek punishment. Have I made myself clear?" No one spoke—no one moved. Remy turned back to Blake. "Now, question the girl! If I decide that more invasive measures need to be taken, I will instruct accordingly."

Invasive measures? My mind wandered back to the needle in my arm and I started to feel nauseous and dizzy again.

Just as Blake was turning back to me, with that evil grin plastered on his face again, Councilman Ash stood up. "Might I try?"

"Excuse me?" Blake asked, as if annoyed by another unwelcome interruption.

"I believe Remy would rather we take a more gentle approach than what you prefer. Perhaps my talents could be of use?" Ash bowed his head, a sign of respect, but not low enough to give Blake the impression that he saw him as anything more than an equal. "Besides, you have already lost someone close to you this evening. I would not want your emotions to dictate your treatment of the girl."

Lost? I was sure he was speaking of Britt, Blake's daughter, but what he meant by lost, I wasn't sure.

"Remy?" Blake asked, not taking his eyes off of Ash.

"Yes, all right. I suppose it couldn't hurt. Perhaps it would save us some time," Remy said, as if he were bored with the whole process already.

Blake reluctantly sat back down in the chair to Remy's left, and Ash pulled his chair forward, placing it directly in front of me. Underneath his calm, expressionless face, Councilman Ash was always thinking and always plotting. I always felt like a lab rat in a laboratory when he looked my way. He certainly never gave off warm and fuzzy vibes, and this time was no different. When he sat down, our knees touched. "Once again, you intrigue me. It is most impressive how you continue to surprise me."

"It is not my—"

"Intention," he said, taking the word right out of my mouth. "I know. Yet, it continues to happen. How do you suppose that is?"

"I don't know, why don't..." As I adjusted in my seat, the needle in my arm tugged, sending a sharp pain through my arm. I closed my eyes and took a deep breath, not wanting to show weakness, and swallowed back the vomit that was threatening to come up. "Why don't you tell *me*? You're a vampire, can't you tell if I'm lying?" I asked.

I knew that most vampires have the ability to sense if someone is telling them the truth or just lying. It has to do with smell, body language, and facial expressions. However, there are some, the really powerful ones, who are like living lie-detectors. They can sense what others cannot. I wasn't sure if Ash had that ability or not, but I guessed—since he had offered to question me, and since Remy agreed—that he did.

"I sense the truth in you, but I feel that you're hiding something as well."

"Aren't we all hiding something?" I asked.

"Touché."

I looked past him, to where the rest of the Council sat, tentatively listening—waiting. "Councilman Ash?" I said, still staring at the others.

"Yes?"

"Can I ask you something?"

"You just did."

That wasn't the response I was expecting. I thought about what I had said and, selecting my words carefully, tried again. "May I ask you another question, please?"

"Go ahead," was all he said.

"The Council doesn't like me very much. You do, but the rest of them don't. Do they?" He was very still, almost unnaturally still even for a vampire. Behind him, the others were uneasy. Serenity shifted in her seat. It was subtle, but I noticed it. Blake smirked; yeah, no subtlety there at all. Even the lycanthropes, Cruz, Donovan, and Phoenix, all looked away. They wouldn't meet my gaze eye to eye. The only ones who seemed comfortable with my question, and not thrown off by it at all, were Remy and Iris.

"What makes you think *I* like you?" he asked.

"I guess you probably don't, but you don't dislike me either. At least not in the same way they dislike me. You are intrigued by me. You've said it too many times for it not to be true, and you can't entirely dislike someone or something that you're that intrigued by." I bit my lip to keep him from noticing the slight tremor that had started. My nerves were starting to get the best of me and I didn't want him to see that. I was hoping my suspicions were accurate. If they were, maybe I could find a way to use that knowledge to get me out of here. Naive? Probably.

"It isn't that they don't like you—"

"*I* don't like her!" Serenity interrupted.

Ash snapped around, and was in her face in seconds, hissing. "Hush! You are not old enough to interrupt me, child."

Interesting, it isn't only me he calls child, I noted to myself.

Then he stood, straightened his jacket, and walked back to where I was sitting. He pulled his chair back and sat down. Our knees no longer touched, and I think that made him, and me, a little more comfortable.

"Don't mind her, Serenity doesn't like anyone."

Behind him, Serenity grunted, as if she wanted to argue but thought better of interrupting again.

"Now, as I was saying, aside from Serenity, it isn't that they don't like you. They just don't understand—"

"Watch yourself," Remy said. He was calm, and yet he commanded attention with the slightest of movements.

Ash took a breath, "You are a vampire. You are also a lycanthrope. We are all trying to understand, which of the two, is your more dominant race."

"My race?"

15

"Yes." he nodded. "Once we have determined if you are more vampire or more lycanthrope, we can determine which laws will govern you."

He seemed content, and sat back in his chair looking almost as smug as he had back during Selection Week, when he learned that I hadn't beaten his record time on the obstacle course. What he had said just now, however—*"Once we have determined if you are more vampire or more lycanthrope, we can determine which laws will govern you."*—repeated itself in my mind again and again. Working as the Vampire Council members' liaison, even if only for a day, I had had access to the laws and regulations governing the sector. I had wondered if vampires and lycanthropes had different sets of rules. It seems, as Councilman Ash just pointed out, that they do. *Interesting,* I thought.

"That's great," I said. "I guess we have something in common then." He just looked at me, unflinching. "I'd like to know what I am too. But that isn't why you sounded the sector alarm, or why Councilman Blake dragged me out of bed. That isn't why I'm tied to this chair either. If that were the case, you never would have released me from Selection Week." I scanned the room and everyone was looking at me now. "You would have tied me up as soon as I was infected with the lycanthrope virus the first time. You never would have let me be released from the Selection Hall. This is something else. There's another reason I'm here, tied up and under scrutiny. Isn't there?"

"You make a valid point."

"Then what is it? Why am I here?" I looked back and Councilman Blake was glaring at me through squinted eyes. I could feel him staring through me as if trying to figure me out, but I was an open book. I had nothing to hide. "Councilman Blake…" I interrupted his trance-like state. "Back in my room, you said something about a murder. Councilman Serenity…" I turned, and she looked up, locking her gaze with mine. "You said it was a vampire who was killed. Who was it?" She didn't answer, not that I really expected her too. "You think I did it, don't you? That's why I'm tied up, right? There must be a reason you all think I'm guilty. So why don't you tell me what happened?" No one answered; no one moved.

When I looked back at Ash, he wore a solemn expression, almost somber. "Why don't you ask me what you really want to know? Ask me if I killed him!" If I could have stood up, I would have. I think it would have given my speech a little more strength, but I was tied to a chair. I wasn't going anywhere.

"Did you kill him?" asked Councilman Ash.

"Who?"

"Did you kill anyone?" he asked, a little more annoyed this time.

"No."

We sat there, Ash and I, eye to eye, for what felt like an eternity. My head started to hurt and it felt as if he were picking at my brain, searching for something that I already knew wasn't there. Then it stopped and, instantly, my head felt better. "She's telling the truth." He stood and turned back to Remy. "Whoever killed Wyatt is still out there."

Wyatt? Wyatt… why does that…? Oh my stars! Wyatt, W351, had been a member of my selection class. We called him *The Coaster*, because he never did more than what was required. He just coasted through life. He kept to himself, not taking sides during arguments, and although he didn't have a lot of close friends no one disliked him. I couldn't imagine anyone who would want to hurt him. He just wasn't the type of guy to make enemies.

"Then the hunt begins. We must search the grounds. They couldn't have gotten far." Remy was out of his seat and starting toward the door.

I needed to know more. "Wait!" I called. "Wyatt? As in W351? He's dead? How? When?" No one bothered to notice that I was still tied to the chair, or that I was asking questions. They just went on talking as if I weren't there, as if I didn't matter anymore.

"Just like that, you trust her? That's all the questioning you feel is appropriate?" Serenity asked, following behind.

"No, I don't trust her, but I do trust Ash. If he says she didn't do it, then she didn't. You know his abilities; you know he would be able to tell if she were lying."

OK, so at least that confirms my suspicions about Ash, but why won't they tell me more about Wyatt?

The Lycanthrope Council members, Cruz, Donovan, Phoenix, and Iris, gathered together as the others began to leave. Then Cruz walked quickly to the doorway and put a hand on the Council Leader's arm. "Remy, if you don't mind, we would like to have a word with you before you go."

"Of course," he nodded, and went with Cruz back to the little group.

"I can't believe this. This is crazy," Serenity interrupted. "Why even get us all together? Why turn this into a Council matter if the opinions of the Council members don't really matter?"

Remy turned and took a step toward her; Serenity didn't back down, but neither did Remy.

"If there is anything more you'd like to say or share with the rest of us, please do so," he said in a quiet tone. "However, I would choose my words wisely if I were you." She didn't respond. "No? Nothing more? Are you sure?" Still no response. Remy turned back to Blake, who was quietly watching from the door. "Blake, I need you to prepare a team. You will lead the hunt. Take Serenity with you, but she isn't to instruct security without you there."

"Excuse me?" Serenity snapped. "Blake is a paper pusher. He sits behind a desk all day and deals with housing and other such nonsense. What does he know about leading a hunt? I can't believe you would—"

Remy grabbed Serenity by the throat and lifted her into the air with her legs dangling. He spoke soft and low. "Councilman Blake was starting wars and destroying colonies long before you were an egg in your mother's uterus. He has chosen to step back from security, but if you keep this up I will gladly put him in charge, for good, and let him show you how it's supposed to be done. Now, do as you've been told."

He released her and turned back to Blake, not bothering to glance back in Serenity's direction, and although she looked pissed she didn't dare raise any further objection.

Remy continued his conversation with Blake as if there had been no interruption. "I don't want word of this to spread, at least not until the moon cycle. If we have no one in custody at that time, we can open the hunt to all sector residents. Until then, select only those you trust. Do you understand?"

"Yes sir," Blake answered.

"What about the nurse?" Serenity asked.

Remy did look at her then. "Nothing has changed. Britt will still be punished." Serenity nodded, and made her way out the door, pushing past Blake without looking back.

Blake, however, remained. "Sir?" he asked, his voice hesitant.

"What is it?" Remy asked.

"I know I don't have any right to ask, but she is my daughter. Is there any possible chance that—?"

"No. I'm sorry old friend, but you must understand where I am coming from. If I show her leniency again, it will be interpreted as weakness. She has had too many opportunities afforded to her already. She must now face the consequences of her actions."

"I understand." Blake turned to go, and I could see that his shoulders slumped a little and his feet dragged along the floor as he walked. In less than a minute, the powerful, commanding demeanor I had grown to associate with Councilman Blake had vanished. For the first time his age, his actual age, was visible on his face, as if the weight of the world rested on his shoulders.

Remy didn't give Blake a second glance as he turned to where Councilman Ash was standing. "Ash, I want you to stay with me. I might have a need for your...talents soon enough." Ash nodded, then returned to his seat across from me, while Remy went to talk with the Lycanthrope Council. "You were saying?"

Cruz stepped forward. "It's the girl. Do you not smell it?"

"You mean the wolf? Yes, I smell it. What of it?"

"It's getting stronger. I—we—can sense it. After tonight, there will only be a few more nights until the moon cycle begins. When the full moon rises on the—"

"I know the cycle of the moon and its possible effects on the girl. Get to your point before..." He interrupted himself to turn and glare at me.

I had been trying to listen to their conversation, while managing to avoid the mind games Ash was still attempting to play on me. Ash spun around and met my gaze, eye to eye. "That was quite a trick," he snarled.

"Excuse me? What trick?" I asked. I could still feel Remy's eyes on me as well, from across the room.

Ash's eyes narrowed. He had been trying to read me, attempting to get back into my mind, but I had been ready this time, and I wasn't going to make it so easy for him again.

21

"We would like permission to keep her in the lycanthrope quarters, under surveillance, during the three nights of the moon cycle," Cruz explained.

I was staring right at Ash, and yet I didn't see him move. "I have a few tricks of my own, you know." He was standing right behind me. He had picked up the fallen gag and now had it wrapped tightly around my throat.

Did he just...he just teleported, didn't he? Did anyone else see that? I thought to myself.

The pressure on my throat was almost unbearable. I gasped for air, struggling not to pass out. "Just try to relax."

3

Try to relax? TRY TO RELAX! Not the best thing to say when you're strangling someone. It actually has the opposite effect. But he was right. If I just allowed myself to relax I would be OK. Other than the irrational human fear of dying, and the discomfort of the gag being so tight against my throat, I was actually fine. It's not like strangling me could really hurt me. It couldn't kill me. You can't kill a vampire just by cutting off their air supply. Besides, I had already developed the ability to go without breathing, unlike most newly formed vampires. Therefore... *Oh my stars, he knows. He knows I don't need to breathe!* The shock of the realization ran through my body. *Is there no way to keep a simple secret from these people?*

"Release her!" Remy said in his soft yet commanding voice.

"She's fine!"

"I said, release her!" This time his voice wasn't so soft and Ash quickly loosened his grip on the gag, allowing it to drop back to the floor at my feet.

Ash leaned in close—too close—and whispered, "I've shown you mine, now you show me yours."

"I don't know what you're talking about," I answered.

He smirked then took a step back. "Very well, but I don't think it will be a secret for much longer." Then, without warning, he was gone—across the room and standing at Remy's side.

He can teleport. Oh my stars, it's true! Ash can teleport. I had no idea teleporting was even possible. I mean, astral projection, sure, I had heard stories. Even visions, heck, in my visions I can actually take control of the other person's body and voice—not very well, but I can do it. But even that wasn't as cool as actually astral projecting, and nowhere near as cool as teleporting.

"You can have the girl, but I want two Council Guard members assigned to watch her," Remy said.

They can have the girl? Me?! What does that mean?

"Which guards did you have in mind?" Donovan asked. Since he is in charge of the external security I had a feeling he had his own plans in mind for me.

"William and Haden."

"But sir, they've been assigned to—"

"I know what they are assigned to do. I assigned them. However, the boy presents no threat to us—yet. So if you want to watch her through the moon cycle, then you will do as I have asked. Otherwise, I won't ask so nicely the next time." He turned to leave, then stopped himself. "Besides, I assume you'll be keeping her in the same place as all the others?"

"Yes, sir."

"Then make sure she and the boy have adjoining cells. I'd like to know what happens when he shifts. Seeing as he is the one who first infected her, having him close by will either push her change as well or ensure that neither of them remains a threat."

"Yes, sir," Donovan agreed.

"As for William and Haden, until the moon cycle starts, they can stay at the Council offices during the day. However, once the moon cycle starts, I want them reassigned to the cells. I want full reports each morning."

The cells? I wondered.

"That would mean 72 hours straight without—"

"If you think it will be too hard on them, or they can't handle it, then they can work in shifts. I have a feeling, though, that neither of them will want to take solitary shifts. Instruct them to take turns feeding, and napping or resting whenever they need to. This task takes precedence. They get along well enough that I don't have to worry about William being in the lycanthrope quarters. Besides, they're both loyal to their respective Councils, so they will keep each other in line around the girl."

I do have a name you know, in case anyone cares. I rolled my eyes, it wouldn't do me any good to—

"The girl has a name," Ash said, as if he had heard my thoughts.

"Excuse me?" Remy said.

Ash looked my way. I could see the confusion in his eyes, but he quickly regained his composure. "I'm sorry, I didn't mean to interrupt. I'm not sure what came over me."

Did I do that? I wondered. When he looked back at me, I just smiled. *I think I actually did that.* I wasn't sure how I had done it, but the look on his face confirmed my suspicion.

Remy dismissed Donovan, and turned back to Cruz. "There will be no harm done to her. However, I want you to instruct William and Haden not to interfere when the boy...changes. Do you understand?" He waited, and so did I, but no one answered. "I will take your silence as a sign of your agreement." He turned to leave. "In Britt's absence, you'll need to take her there tonight."

"Tonight?" Councilman Phoenix asked the question that was burning in my mind at that very instant. "But the moon cycle doesn't start for another three nights. I need to prepare the holding cells—"

Holding cells? Wow, this just keeps getting better and better.

"She can stay with me." Councilman Iris spoke up quickly, before Remy had a chance to respond. "Just until the holding cells are ready for everything. We don't usually lock them up until the moon cycle actually starts."

"Fine, but as I said—" Remy glared back over his shoulder at Phoenix "—make sure that she and the boy have adjoining cells. I'm interested to see how his wolf reacts to her. Until then, she can stay with Councilman Iris."

"Very well," Phoenix replied, and then he and Ash were gone.

I sat there, still tied to the chair, with the four Lycanthrope Council members glaring at me from the other side of the room. If I could have dug a hole to hide in I would have, but seeing as I was *tied to a chair*, with no escape plan, all I could do was wait.

"We could just kill her now. One less vampire in the sector wouldn't bother me one bit," Councilman Donavan said, breaking the silence.

"No, we will do as Remy has instructed," Cruz interjected. "Then, after the moon cycle, when she proves to be lycanthrope, we will petition the Council to assign her to the lycanthrope quarters permanently."

They all stared at him in disbelief, but only Iris spoke up. "And you think they'll go for that?"

"Not in the least, but there won't be any way to deny what she is at that point; and besides, the physical demands on newly changed lycanthropes far outweigh those of a vampire. We can manage her thirst, but they would have no way to control her changes. They would have to give in eventually anyway. Besides, the boy managed a partial change while fighting her on the mat, and that was nowhere near the start of the moon cycle. Who knows, maybe he will develop the ability of selective shifting."

"Selective shifting…you really think so?" Donavan asked.

"It's been a while since we've had a lycanthrope that powerful, but yes, I think it's possible. And if *he* can do it, maybe she can too." He was staring right at me and all I wanted at that moment was to get up and run away—far, far away.

Councilman Phoenix threw back his head and laughed. It seemed so foreign against his stern features. He is a small man, with wiry brown hair that stands straight up about an inch, a thin mustache, and a five-o'clock shadow that never seems to go away. It's funny how lycanthropes start to resemble the beast they carry inside, or maybe he's always looked like a hyena.

I closed my eyes and took a few deep breaths, waiting for them to approach, but they never did. Eventually Councilman Phoenix's laughter faded away, and when I opened my eyes it was just Councilman Iris and me, alone in the room. Iris has always had a soft, reassuring demeanor. Her hazel eyes often fade to a pale green and her brown hair, although dark, somehow seems to bring a brightness to her face that resembles the soft glow of the moon.

I wasn't sure why the others had left, but I wasn't going to complain about it either. I had known Councilman Iris all my life. Up until recently, Selection Week to be exact, I would have listed her as one of the people I trusted most in life. Iris is in charge of Sector C's selection student resources, and up until Selection Week all the students in our selection class tended to think of her as a personal mentor. I've been turning to her with all my non-academic issues since as far back as I can remember. However, once I became a vampire my list of trusted individuals seemed to shrink substantially. Considering that newly changed vampires are not allowed to mingle with, or even talk to, the lycanthrope sector members it's hard to know if you can still trust them. However, I'm an exception, or so it seems.

"A53." She smiled, addressing me as if I were still a selection student coming to her for advice.

"It's Zelina now."

"Of course, I'm sorry." She sat down in the same chair that Councilman Ash had previously occupied. Her eyes sparkled affectionately as she smiled at me. It was not at all like the challenging independence one might expect to see in someone staring into the eyes of a tiger out in the wild, and yet there was something of that there too. "Although, it was a surprising choice—Zelina, I mean. It's a very lovely name. Do you know what it means?"

Why is she not untying me?

"No, do you?"

"I do. It is an ancient Greek word meaning zealous."

"Zealous?"

"Yes." She smiled. "It means to be passionately and enthusiastically active in the service of some ideal, sometimes even fanatically so."

We sat there for a while as I contemplated the meaning. "Why do I get the feeling you don't think that is a good thing?" I finally ventured.

"No, I didn't say that. It's actually quite the opposite. I believe the name suits you. You are indeed passionate and enthusiastic. I think if given the opportunity and the proper guidance you could do great things. Sometimes that takes someone with a little fanaticism."

"Then why are you afraid of me?"

"I'm not af—"

"Yes, you are." I cut her off. "Otherwise you would have untied me by now."

She looked back at the door that was now closed—symbolically, if not literally, trapping us both inside. "How rude of me. I apologize, I should have untied you before I sat down." She stood and made her way to my chair and untied the rope that bound my left wrist, then moved to the right side. "This might hurt a bit, but I'll need to pull the IV out. Are you ready?"

I nodded, because I wasn't able to answer with my teeth clenched tightly in anticipation of the pain.

"On three. One, two—"

"Ouch," I screamed as she pulled the tape off, and the needle out, all at once—on two, not three.

"Sorry, I thought it might be easier if it was a surprise."

"Yeah, no. Not easier."

Once my arms were both untied and needle-free, I bent forward and untied my legs. Standing and stretching felt better than I expected. I hadn't realized how tight the ropes had been until I felt the blood rushing back into my hands and feet. It didn't hurt exactly, but it was definitely uncomfortable. Iris sat back down and waited for me to finish. "Are you all right with the idea of staying with me?" she asked.

"Um, I guess. It doesn't really matter though, does it?"

"No, I suppose it doesn't, but I'd like you to be all right with it." She said it and I actually believed she meant it.

"Are you all right with it?" I had no idea why she would be; I am a vampire, after all, and not one in total control of her cravings yet.

"I am. As I said, I think that with the right guidance you could—"

"Do great things, yeah. And you believe you're the one to guide me to said greatness?"

"I think I'm a good place to start. You've spent the last two weeks learning about your vampire half, and it seems you're quite a fast learner. However, I think that it's time you stopped suppressing your wolf and your lion."

She sounded an awful lot like Merick at the moment. "Well, you're not the only one who's told me that lately. So maybe there is some truth to it."

"Really?" She cocked her head to the side and a sweet smile caressed her lips. "May I ask who?"

It's funny because until that moment I hadn't realized just how much being a vampire had changed me. Sure, there was the whole drinking blood thing, but this was different. All my life Iris had been someone I trusted, relied on, even confided in. Yet, something inside of me was urging me not to answer, not to bring Merick into this, as if I needed to protect him.

"It doesn't matter," I answered, hoping she would drop it, and she did.

"All right."

Hmm, that was easy, almost too easy. "So now what?" I asked.

"Now we go home. If you're ready, that is."

"Ready to get out of here? Yes! What time is it anyway? I feel like I haven't slept all night."

"You have slept, or at least rested. What did you think the IV was for?"

"Um, I—"

"Medically induced rest never really feels like sleep. Don't worry, the effects will wear off soon enough."

31

I looked over at the IV bag hanging from the pole next to my seat, but it was already empty. I squinted, but couldn't make out the tiny words on the back of the clear plastic bag. *Medically induced rest?* I wondered what that meant, and why they had felt the need to do it.

What the fuck did you people inject me with? Is what I wanted to say, but what came out was, "What was it? What was in the IV?"

"Nothing that will hurt you. Just a sedative, something to relax you."

A sedative, great. "So, what time is it then?"

"Seven forty-five."

"Are you kidding? Seven forty-five? I should be ready for work and heading to the Council offices right now." I looked down at my own internal monitor, and she was right. They had pulled me out of my room around three in the morning. That meant that they had kept me here for almost four hours. "I've been here nearly four hours? Why? How is that even possible? Was anything even accomplished, other than making me lose feeling in my hands and feet?"

"Your absence at the Council offices today will not be held against you. However, you misunderstood. It is seven forty-five in the evening. It's been almost seventeen hours. And yes, we accomplished a great deal while you were..." She contemplated her words. "While you were resting. We also established your innocence, which I would think you would be relieved about."

"Yes, I am." She did have a point. "What do you mean you accomplished a great deal while I was resting? How?"

"You were not the only reason we were gathered here. We had other matters to attend to as well."

"Other matters? You mean Britt, don't you?"

She didn't answer. I'm not sure I wanted to know anyway. "I'm surprised you made it this long without feeding. We should probably get you something to drink before your thirst becomes unmanageable."

Unmanageable? She made it sound like feeding my thirst was the same as dealing with frizzy hair on a humid day.

"Come to think of it, I am pretty hungry." Hunger is different now. Now that my body has changed, I no longer get that deep rumbling in my stomach when I've gone too long between meals. Now, the burning in my throat reminds me when it's time to eat. I'm not sure I would even consider what I do, what vampires do, as eating. No, feeding— *feeding* seems more appropriate.

"I can already see in your eyes that you need to feed. I would rather not be the one you feed on if I can help it."

"Yeah, no. I would rather not *feed* on you either."

"What? Why? Is my blood not good enough for you?"

I had meant for it to be reassuring, but apparently she hadn't taken it that way. "That's not what I meant. I just...I'm just trying to avoid eating my friends is all." A flashback to that first dinner I spent in the dining hall with Britt popped into my mind, and I shuddered.

33

"That's your friends you're smelling. So, unless you want them for dinner, I suggest we go upstairs." I had a feeling Britt's warning would be haunting me for years to come.

"At least you see me as a friend. I think that's progress," she said. "Shall we go?" She headed for the door, not waiting for my reply. I think she wanted out of that room as much as I did.

4

As we made our way through the sector, we passed one of the Council's large communication screens that are used to display video of Council announcements. Neither the meeting hall nor the courtyard outside of the Selection Week Building is large enough to hold everyone in the sector, and there are times when the Council has mandatory announcements that must be attended by everyone. The communication screens, placed throughout the sector, permit residents to view ordinary updates whenever it is convenient for them, and make it possible for everyone to be present in one way or another for the occasional mandatory announcements. Tonight, the screens were displaying typical everyday information: the time, the date, and the current Sector C population count.

"35,759."

"What?" Iris asked, as she stopped and turned back to see what I had said.

Did I say that out loud?

"The population count; it dropped again. 35,759, it was 35,761 when I saw it last. If only Wy..." It was hard saying his name, knowing that he was dead. "If only Wyatt died..."

Iris stared up at the screen.

OK, no, it wasn't a question, but I was expecting a response.

Finally, she looked away from the screen. "It's not only death that causes the population count to drop. You know that."

"You mean Britt?"

"Come on, we need to get moving," Iris said as she started back down the street.

That was it. Britt had been banished from Sector C. Her monitor had been turned off and now…now she was no longer a part of our population count. It was as easy as that, and you no longer counted. It felt so final. As I followed Iris down the road, I wondered how Blake must be feeling.

The closer we got to the lycanthrope section, the more I could feel people watching us—watching me. The curfew wouldn't start for another hour, but the mood in the air seemed to be shifting. The sky was already dark, but the yellowish-orange glow from the streetlights, every forty feet, made it look lighter than it really was. "What's selective shifting?"

"What?" Iris asked, not stopping to look back.

"Selective shifting. Councilmen Cruz mentioned it. I was just wondering what it means."

"It's when a lycanthrope has the ability to complete a partial transformation, without having to shift entirely into their animal form."

"A partial transformation…you mean, like shifting just their face, or…" I remembered the way M had dug his claws into me during our fight. I remembered how surprised everyone had been. "…or their claws?"

36

"Yes. That's what I mean. Usually, a partial transformation occurs as a form of self-defense, but it is very rare. Not many lycanthropes have the ability anymore."

"Do you?" I asked.

Her shoulders stiffened and there was a slight pause in her step. "No."

"Oh." If that was true, if selective shifting really is rare, and they really did believe that M might develop the aptitude for partial transformations, then he might be in danger. I pushed the thought aside; there was nothing I could do at that moment. I did make a mental note to talk to M about it later, though. "So, do I get to pick up my things from Britt's place, or am I just supposed to wear my pajamas for the rest of the week? Cause I think people are starting to notice."

"Your things have already been moved."

"They've what? Who moved them?"

"It doesn't matter," she said, as if having a total stranger going through her things wouldn't have pissed her off.

"It matters to me!"

"Britt packed them up herself before they—" She stopped. I couldn't tell if she was thinking, or listening.

"Before what?"

She didn't answer right away. "Before they took her into custody."

"Oh." Apparently Britt's testimony hadn't gone well. If she had been taken into custody by the Council, there was only one of two punishments she could be facing: banishment from the sector, or death. I already knew that the population count had dropped, but I didn't think I should ask if it was due to her death or her banishment.

"I got the master access card from Councilman Blake and had a friend pick up your things from Britt's place and deliver them to my apartment."

"A friend of yours…or a friend of mine?"

She stopped and turned toward me. "Who says they can't be one and the same?"

"I hardly think—" I was about to tell her that wasn't possible, but then I saw him—no, I *felt* him— Merick. He was close, but when I spun around, searching the street and nearby buildings, I couldn't see him anywhere. I closed my eyes and focused on his smile, his smell, and his lips.

Iris stepped back. "Zelina, are you all right?"

"Shhh, I'm all right." I held a finger to my lips as if shushing a child. I'm certain Iris didn't like the gesture, but she stayed quiet just the same. *M, is that you?* I asked, not out loud, but I was sure he would still hear me.

Hey, I was wondering when you were gonna get here.

Here?

Iris's place. I've been waiting for the last two hours.

I'm coming.

I broke our connection and quickly opened my eyes, searching for the right direction. It was as if I had finally gotten my second wind. The fact that I had been awoken at three in the morning, drugged, and then interrogated didn't seem to matter anymore. "We should go!" I told Iris, and quickly started walking.

"Go where?"

"Your place." I headed down the road, and I could hear M's voice in my head. This time he wasn't actually talking to me; he was sending me a memory of the tour he had given me the night before.

"The were-bears live over in those buildings, the tigers and the lions are down that street and the wolves live over here, by the park."

Before I turned left down the road I knew Iris must live on, I glanced back at the park. It had only been twenty-four hours since I was there with M, and already so much had happened.

I couldn't get to him fast enough. I hurried down the road with Iris close behind. "Zelina! Zelina, you've passed it," she called out, as my tunnel vision led me farther down the road.

"I what?" Turning around, I saw Iris standing in the center of the street, about thirty feet back. "Oh, sorry."

As I trotted back to her, she cocked her head, staring at me with a quizzical look on her face, as if she were trying to solve a mystery I didn't even know existed. "Where's the fire?"

"Um, I don't know what you mean."

"Don't you?" She nodded toward her building and I followed as she headed for the door. "How did you know this was my street?"

"I…um. Don't all the werelions and weretigers live down this street?" I asked, as if it were common knowledge—which it probably is for anyone who isn't a newly-graduated vampire selection student.

"Yeah, they do, but how did *you* know that?"
Busted!

"You know I'm the Vampire Council liaison." I left it at that. I hoped that she would think that because of my position I was privy to information that other new vampire graduates weren't, such as sector maps. Besides, I'm sure I am, I just haven't seen them yet. *Note to self, study the sector maps if they ever let me back into the Council building again.*

"Oh, and I thought it was because you and Merick took your own little private tour of the sector last night." Iris smiled as she turned and made her way into the building, leaving me behind with my jaw on the ground.

I picked my jaw up off the ground and hustled after her. Her door was the first one on the left. As she started to unlock the door I started to feel nervous, anxious, and even a bit scared. "Wait." I wanted to go in, quickly, and yet I wanted to run.

She pulled her access card out of the card reader and turned to look back at me. "What's wrong?"

"I—I don't know. Can we *not* go in yet?"

"A few minutes ago you couldn't get here fast enough; now you don't want to go in?"

She was right. Only a few minutes ago I was rushing down the road to get to Merick, who, I knew, was waiting inside. I could feel him there behind the door. I could hear his heartbeat and taste his lips as if they were inches from my own. However, standing there at her door, I couldn't help but feel like, if I went inside, something bad would happen. That I might do something bad.

"I'm sorry. I can't explain it, I just…I need…"

"You're hungry, you just need to feed."

Is that all it is? Is it just hunger? I'm sure I was hungry, but I didn't think that was all it was. There was something more, something pulling me toward her apartment, something that didn't feel right or natural. I wanted to go inside with every ounce of my being, and that feeling alone made me not want to go in. I was afraid that, with Merick inside, my hunger—or something worse—would make me do something I didn't mean to do. I wasn't feeling *welcomed* by Merick. I was feeling *pulled* to him.

M...

I'm here.

You can't stay. It isn't safe.

But—

Please.

Iris put her arm around my waist. "I have some bottled blood in my refrigerator. I think if you just come inside and have a drink, you'll feel better." She started back toward her door with her access card out and ready, but I stopped her again.

"Can I ask you something?" I'm not sure if I was buying time or if I really cared. All I do know is that I couldn't go into that apartment—not with Merick still inside.

"Of course."

"Why did you offer to take me in? Why did you want to help me?"

"Like I said, I believe I can help you. Zelina, I've known you all your life. Just because you're a vampire doesn't mean that our friendship—all those times you came to me for help—doesn't mean anything anymore. I'm still the same person you confided in. The same person you've trusted all your life. Besides, I know you almost as well as you know yourself, but what you don't know about yourself, the part that I can help you with, is your beast."

"My beast?"

"That's what we lycanthropes call our animal forms. Lycanthropes are never just human or just animal. Sure, we live as humans the majority of the time, but our animals, our beasts, are alive within us twenty-four hours a day, seven days a week. That is true for you as well, even though you are also a vampire. Once you learn to not only control but to understand and even listen to your beast, you will be able to understand who you really are."

"You mean *what* I am."

She gave her head a firm shake. "No, not what, who."

At that moment, I heard a door open down the hall. "Iris, is that you?" It was one of her neighbors.

"Yeah, sorry if we were too loud."

"No, it's fine. I was just—" He turned the corner and stopped, staring straight at me. "What are you doing with a vampire in the building?"

"She isn't—"

"Even if everyone in Sector C didn't already know who she is, I can smell it on her."

Iris quickly turned back to her door and swiped the access card through the reader and unlocked the door. "I think we should continue this inside, Zelina." She pushed me in and closed the door. I heard her muffled voice as she spoke to the man down the hall. "I've been assigned by the Council to take care of the girl. You won't even know she's here." Then she joined me inside and locked the door behind her.

"Everything OK?" I asked.

"Of course."

I could tell she wasn't going to give me any more details on her own, but maybe if I asked? "Who was that?"

"After you have something to drink we can finish our conversation. OK?" I tried to smile, but nothing happened.

"Yeah, sure."

Why was he so upset that I was in the building? I wondered for a moment. *Oh wait, I'm a vampire in a lycanthrope building. Why wouldn't he be upset?*

I could feel my heart pounding in my chest as if someone were about to jump out and scare me, but nothing happened. We walked into the empty living room and Iris nodded toward the couch. "Why don't you sit down. I'll get you a drink, and we can talk some more."

I did as she asked, and waited.

M? M, are you there? I could *feel* him. I could *smell* him, that sweet, clean scent I've grown to like so much—to need. *Merick?* It was the strangest feeling; I knew he had been there only moments before—it had been Merick that I had been drawn to. Yet, he wasn't here. He had listened to me—he had left. Suddenly, I wanted him back. *Why did I tell him to go? I would never have hurt him, not intentionally. I— no.* I wasn't ready to admit how I felt about him. Not even to myself.

"Here, drink this." Iris had returned and was holding out a glass of freshly poured blood. Seeing the thick, red liquid through the clear glass just didn't seem right. "Did you want a straw?" she asked. I must have been staring at the glass for longer than I thought.

"No. No thank you." I took the glass. "It's just…I've never actually seen it before. I always drink it out of the dark bottles it comes in. I guess…not seeing it kind of makes it easier."

Iris took a small step back. "Oh, I'm sorry, I didn't know. If you would like, I can pour it back—"

"No, I'm fine, really. I mean, this is part of my life now, right? I just need to get used to it."

5

We sat in the living room and Iris stared at me while I drank the blood. *Yeah, that doesn't make it any less awkward.* Once I was finished, I politely wiped my lips. Sometimes the thirst takes over and drinking can become a little messy. The last thing I needed was to freak her out on the first night I stayed in her apartment.

"Do you need more?"

"No thank you." I put the glass down on the table in front of the couch and sat back. It felt good to finally relax. I felt like I hadn't had a good night's sleep in forever. "So who was that guy? The one out in the hall?"

She shifted in her seat glancing back at the door as if he could hear us. "That was Dominic. He is the Sway of the Sector C tigers."

"The sway?"

"They didn't teach you lycanthrope hierarchy in your classes, did they?"

"No, not really."

"It's a title: Sway. It identifies him as the leader. Tigers, unlike most other lycanthropes, don't really have packs or prides. We hunt alone and take care of ourselves. Rarely will you find a weretiger in a

45

relationship, but it does happen." She stopped talking and was fiddling with her gold arrow bracelet, the one that marks her as a member of the Council.

"How did he become the leader?"

It seemed like a simple question, but the expression on her face when she looked up was anything but simple. "Like all other leaders within the lycanthrope world, he killed for it. The lycanthropy virus slows down the aging process, but we aren't immortal. We do die when we get old enough, and of course we can be killed. Most lycanthrope leaders don't die of natural causes or old age, though. Becoming the leader in the lycanthrope world means you also become a target. Your own people will fight you, to take control, but in order for there to be an actual change in power, the old leader must—"

"Die?"

"Yes."

"If he's the leader, why isn't he on the Council?"

"He was, but he didn't get along with the others, so he assigned me as his representative." She looked up and smiled. "I get along with everyone."

That smile was mischievous, calculating. It made me wonder aloud, "Has there ever been a female leader?"

"Not in Sector C, but there's a first for everything, right?" She was still smiling. I knew what she was thinking without even needing to ask. She planned to be the first female Sway in Sector C.

We sat there in silence for a few minutes as I looked around, taking in the room for the first time. She lived pretty sparsely; there was not a lot of furniture, and the walls were bare. While I was looking around, she was watching me. I could feel her eyes on me, like a weight placed upon my shoulders. I wasn't ready to go to bed—the blood I had drunk had given me a boost of energy. If I could have, I would have gone out for a run, but I really didn't think Iris was going to agree to that. Instead, I kept talking.

"So, if the tigers are different, like you said, how do the other lycanthropes work?"

She sat back in her chair and crossed her arms, finally relaxing. "This could be a long night," she said, but she was smiling, so I guessed it didn't bother her. "The wolves run in packs, with a male Alpha in charge. His…mate, or rather wife or lover here in Sector C, since we aren't allowed to procreate, is called the Lupa."

"Lupa? What does that mean?"

"It's Latin for she-wolf. In the werewolf hierarchy, it refers to the dominant female wolf, who is always the one taken to wife by the Alpha."

"Taken? You mean she doesn't have a choice?"

Iris just laughed. "Trust me, all the female werewolves want to be the Lupa. They fight for that position just like the males fight to be the Alpha. It's seen as an honor, not a punishment. As the Lupa, they are second in command of the pack and, although the Alpha has the final say on all matters and decisions of the Pack, the Lupa has his ear more so than any of the others."

"So an Alpha is always a male?"

"Yes, always, but there isn't only one Alpha in Sector C. We have a number of wolf packs here; I'm not even sure how many. Each pack has an Alpha and a Lupa." She got up and started toward the kitchen. "I'm going to get something to eat. Would you like anything else?"

"No. Wait, yes please. Can I have another glass of...?" Saying the word blood makes me almost as nauseous as the idea of drinking it does, but it does taste good.

"Sure thing."

Thank you, for not making me say it, I thought to myself.

"Then there are the bears," Iris continued from inside the kitchen. "They also form packs, but they call them companies or sloths. Not a great name, but I guess it suits them, seeing as unless they're fighting, hunting, or on guard duty, they do tend to be pretty lazy. Actually, sometimes even while they're on guard duty they're pretty lazy." She laughed, but quickly stopped herself. "Their leader is called the Ursus and his mate the Parum-Ursa, the little bear.

"The lion packs are called prides. Lions are one of the few lycanthrope breeds that are female-led. The dominant lion is called the Leaena or Lioness."

"Does the Leaena have a male counterpart?" She knew what I was asking—does she take a mate—but she still paused, watching me carefully.

"Are you asking because of the lion you carry inside of you or...?"

"No," I insisted, because I wasn't. *Was I?* In all honesty, as a general rule I tried not to think of the lion or the wolf I carry inside of me.

"She can, but she doesn't always. The males often stay to themselves. Here in Sector C, most of the werelions are female. For whatever reason, the lion lycanthropy virus that's been created doesn't survive well in males. That's why it's rare when a male Selection Student is injected with—"

"Hudson," I interrupted. "Why would they inject Hudson with lion lycanthrope virus if they didn't think he would survive?"

"The selection process is more complicated than you can imagine, Zelina. But, to put it simply, the leaders of all the different lycanthropy breeds throughout the sector review each of the students who have selected the lycanthropy injection. Prior to administration of the injections, the leaders are given the opportunity to choose who, if any, of the students, they wish to join their pack, pride, sloth—whatever. Hudson was no different. He was chosen, by the Leaena."

Hudson, formerly H107, was the youngest in our selection class. At the end of Selection Week, Remy, the Sector Leader, had announced Hudson as a werelion. Thinking back, I remember how the crowd had sat there in silence as the boy was formally presented to the group. No one had said a word until after Teagan announced that Hudson's job assignment was as a Selection Counselor-in-training.

Teagan had made the announcement, not Remy.

"Who is the Leaena?"

Iris hesitated, too long.

"Teagan?"

"Yes. Why?"

It all made sense. Teagan had picked Hudson, just like she had picked Micah when she was in

Sector M. I wanted to ask if it was her blood that was used in the injection, but I didn't. I trusted Iris, but I wasn't sure I trusted her enough to expose all of my curiosities just yet.

I changed the subject.

"So, how did you know that Merick and I had spent time together, last night I mean?" It had only been the one time.

"He told me."

"He told you? When?"

"Earlier today, while you were being detained. I ran into him in the hallway at the Council office. I couldn't tell him what was happening, but he said you weren't in the office. I think he was worried about you. He volunteered the information, said he had shown you around. He had already told me how he felt about you, previously, and he knew I would be happy for the two of you."

"I—Oh."

"Don't worry, Zelina. Merick trusts me, and so can you." She had been sipping tea, but took that moment to set her cup down on the table between us. "Many of the newly graduated selection students come to me after they change. At least the lycanthrope students do. Merick, like the others—like you, sometimes just needs someone to talk to. Someone who understands what they're going through. Since I'm a familiar face, I think it's just easier to come to me than to their assigned mentor."

"Mentor?"

"Like Britt was for you."

"Britt was no mentor," I snapped. *OK, maybe that was too harsh.* "What I mean to say is…"

"It's all right, you don't need to explain. It's no secret how Britt felt about you. However, even though you didn't see her as a mentor, and even though she was afraid of you, she did still try to teach you."

"Wait, did you say she was afraid of me?"

"I did." She was silent for a minute, but I waited. I knew there was more she wasn't telling me. "Back at the Council office, you said that the Council members don't like you. That isn't entirely accurate. It's not that we don't like you, and it isn't just that we don't understand you either. A few of us, myself included, as well as many throughout the sector, are curious about you. The others, they fear you—what you can do or will be able to do. But there are those among us, and many throughout the sector, who believe you might actually be the answer we've been seeking."

"The answer to what?"

Iris took a deep breath as if contemplating something. "To the ongoing war between the lycanthropes and the vampires, of course. We believe you could help end it, forever."

The answer to the war between the lycanthropes and the vampires? Yeah, no pressure there.

"How could I be the answer, I'm just—"

"You are far from being *just* a child," she said, not waiting for me to finish.

"I wasn't going to say 'a child.' I know I'm not a child." OK, so maybe that's a sore spot for me. "I was going to say that I'm just one person. How can one person stop a war?"

"There is so much I want—*need*—to share with you. So much you haven't learned yet. However, I don't believe now is the time or the place to discuss what your future may or may not bring. Right now, I think you should rest. I had hoped Merick would be here to greet you, but it seems he had to leave. I'm sure he will stop by in the morning to check in on you." She stood, waiting for me to follow, then made her way through the kitchen and toward a staircase that led to the bedrooms on the second floor. "That fridge is fully stocked with everything you'll need. Feel free to help yourself. Come along now, I'll show you to your room. I think you'll feel better after you get a full night's sleep."

I didn't say anything; I just followed her up the stairs and into a small, cozy room at the back of the apartment. What few belongings I had were already there. My pictures had been hung on the wall, my clothes were hanging in the closet, and my books were already placed on the shelves along the far wall. "It's…"

"It's small, I know. But, hopefully, you'll feel comfortable here."

"I do. I mean, I will. Thank you."

"The bathroom is right down the hall if you need it."

"What's going to happen to Britt? I mean, I know they interrogated her, too. You said they took her into custody, does that mean…?"

"Do you really want to know?"

I stared at her for a while. I had asked the question. I had thought I wanted to know, but maybe I didn't. Maybe I wouldn't be able to handle knowing the truth. "I…" *I don't know.* "Yes."

"Britt has been sent away."

"You mean…the Council has banished her? From the sector?"

"Yes. We allowed her to collect some of her personal belongings, which is more than we typically permit, then the guards took her to the wall and released her."

"I—"

"Try not to think about it. I'd like to tell you it gets easier, but it doesn't. Even though Britt and I didn't get along, it isn't a fate I would ever have wished for her. Although, the alternative would have been much worse." With that, she left me to my thoughts.

There was an envelope on the dresser with my name on it. I picked it up, looking back over my shoulder, wondering if Iris had left it for me or if it was from Britt. I quickly tore it open. Only a picture slid out. It was of Merick and me, in the woods, sitting on top of the ten-foot warp wall. We weren't doing anything wrong, at least not that could be seen through a camera lens. We were just sitting there, looking down at the ground below us.

I remembered the moment, as if it were yesterday, although at the time I had no idea anyone was watching, let alone taking our photo. Had the photograph captured more of the area below us, Hudson would have been in the picture too. It was the first time the three of us had run the Selection Week obstacle course together. It had taken Hudson almost an hour to make it up and over the warp wall, but

Merick and I didn't care. We were in our own little world up there. I would gladly go back to that day—to that moment. If only that were possible…

"Whatcha thinking about?" I quickly turned to the door, but no one was there. "Behind you." When I turned to the window, Merick was standing there just in front of it, hands on his hips, smiling. "Is this OK?"

I didn't answer him, at least not with words. I ran into his arms and he quickly wrapped them around me. "I've missed you so much." *Wait, I'm on the second floor.* I quickly pulled back a little and looked out the window, down to the ground below us. There wasn't a ladder, or even a vine running up the side of the wall. "How did you—?"

"Perks of being a lycanthrope," he said, with a smile on his face.

Oh, that smile. Then I was back in his tight embrace.

"I've missed you too. It feels like I haven't seen you in—"

"Days? I know."

"What happened to you today? You didn't show up at the Council office, and then I ran into Iris in the hall and she asked me to pick up all your things from Nurse Britt's house and bring them here. It was weird; she was all cryptic and secretive. I was worried that the sector alarms last night had something to do with the reason you…"

"Iris really didn't tell you?"

"Tell me what?"

"The Council, or rather Councilman Blake, dragged me out of bed last night and took me to the Council offices. They interrogated both Britt and me all night. They kept me there, tied to a chair for over sixteen hours. And Britt—they're banishing her from Sector C."

"They what?" He pulled away and headed for the door.

"Don't! It won't do any good. Besides, it's over, and I'm pretty sure Iris is on my side."

He stood there with his hand on the doorknob, fighting not to walk out.

"Merick, sit down, please."

I could tell he didn't want to, but he eventually released his grip on the doorknob and made his way back to my side. Sitting there on the bed, so close to him, I could feel the heat radiating from his body. My brain started sorting through what I had learned about lycanthropes during my studies: increased body temperature was normal. It was one of the distinct differences between lycanthropes and vampires, and something that made being close to him even more intoxicating.

Merick's hands tightened into fists. "Did they hurt you?" He wouldn't even look at me.

"No. Not unless you count the rope burns I got from being tied down, but even those didn't really hurt, and they've already started to heal. See." I lifted my hands to show him and there was only a faint red line along my wrists.

"What did they want?"

"They wanted to know if I—If I was the one who killed Wyatt."

Then, he did look at me. "Wyatt's dead? What happened?"

"I'm not sure. They wouldn't tell me, but they know it was a vampire who killed him. That's why they thought it was me. Britt had told them I came home with blood—she told them I had fed. Unsupervised. She didn't know it was—"

"My blood."

"Right."

He pulled me into his lap and held my face in his hands. We were so close I could feel his breath on my lips. "Oh my stars, A, I'm so sorry. I never meant for you to—"

"M, it's not your fault. I should never have done it in the first place. It's no one's fault but my own."

He was shaking his head, and his eyes were sad and pleading. "Don't say that."

"Say what?"

"That it shouldn't have happened. It was…amazing. I don't regret it one bit. I don't know why, but I feel—closer to you somehow. Like I'm drawn to you, more than I already was. That's why I couldn't stay away tonight. That's why I came back even after you told me to leave. I just, I wish I had known what was happening to you today. I had this awful feeling all day, but I didn't know what it was. If I had only known. I would have done something. I would have helped."

I laughed, not because he was funny or because I didn't believe him, but because he was so sincere, so loving and honest. I wasn't sure I really knew how to respond to that. Merick had always been the class clown, the jokester. Seeing him this way was just another sign of how much we had changed over the last few weeks. "There was nothing you could have done. Besides, like I said, they didn't hurt me. More importantly, I didn't do what they thought I did. They know that now, so I'm OK."

"Yeah."

I realized, sitting there on his lap, I still had the photo of the two of us, on top of the warp wall, clutched tightly in my hand. "Hey, how did you get this picture?"

"What picture?"

"This one." I held up the picture and he took it, smiling. "It was on my dresser in an envelope. I figured you put it there when you brought all my things from Britt's house.

"A, I've never seen this photo before. Wait..." His smile faded—darkened. "Who took this?"

"I don't know. I hadn't really thought about—"

"A, this is when we were on the course with H—I mean Hudson. My stars it's difficult getting used to using everyone's new *names*." He turned to me and it was as if the color had drained right out of him. He was staring right at me but wasn't looking at me at all. "This was before Selection Week. This was when—"

"When they were watching us."

"Why would someone leave this for you now?"

It was as if, instantly, I knew. "Because they're still watching us."

"Shit." The weight of it all sank in and he dropped to the bed.

"Yeah—shit."

We sat there on the bed, inches apart, for what felt like an eternity before he broke the silence that threatened to suffocate us. "So Wyatt's really dead?"

"That's what they said."

"And they don't know who did it?"

"No, not yet. But Remy called for a hunt. They're probably out there right now scouring the sector."

He pulled back and a single tear rolled down his face. "A, he was one of us. They don't prepare you for what really happens after Selection Week. What if it had been you? What if—?"

"Do you remember—" I interrupted him, because I knew where his thoughts were about to take him "—during the Selection Week ceremony, how Wyatt took the stage and walked straight up to Councilman Remy like the Sector *Leader* was just another resident? I had no idea Wyatt was going to select vampirism. He never had a preference, at least not that I knew. I actually thought that maybe Wyatt and T...T...what name did she pick?" I asked.

"Tamsin."

"Right, Tamsin. I almost thought he and Tamsin might end up dating after the ceremony. They both selected vampirism, and I knew he had liked her for a while. I guess that didn't work out, huh?"

"I guess not," he said, without looking up. "It wouldn't have worked out anyway."

"Why?" I asked.

"You know T. As soon as she heard he had been assigned as a service worker she wrote him off, if he was even ever really on her radar in the first place."

"Yeah, I guess you're right." I thought about that for a second. All our lives we were programmed not to get too close to each other, at least not in a romantic way. With the Selection Week decision we all would have to make—the inevitable decision out there on our horizons—it just didn't make sense to get too attached to someone, but that didn't mean we didn't have crushes. "Do you think...?"

"What?"

"I was just wondering, do you think anyone— besides us I mean—ever acted on their...you know."

"Crushes?"

Crushes?

"Is that all we are?" I asked.

"No, no of course not. You know that's not how I feel. I just meant... Never mind. Yes, I'm pretty sure others in our class and classes before and after ours, acted on their *feelings*, for lack of a better word." With his arm around my waist, he pulled me even closer to his side. The warmth of his body radiated off of him like my own little space heater. I felt as safe, there with him, as I ever had.

"I was so nervous that day. I remember, hearing Remy call my name when it was my turn to go up on stage, and I tried, I swear I did, but I just couldn't get up. I'm not even sure how many times he called me, but I—"

"Twice," Merick answered, without being asked. "It was twice."

"Twice," I repeated. "His voice felt like it was so far away. I don't even remember walking up to the stage. One second I was sitting in my chair, trying to convince myself to get up, and the next I was standing there next to Councilman Remy, staring out at what seemed like the whole world, waiting for my punishment."

"Punishment?" he asked.

"I was sure he was going to banish me, or worse. Then, when he read my lab results in front of everyone, he made me a target; everyone saw me as a monster—an abomination. I think that was even worse, having to defend myself. I thought..." I wiped a tear from my cheek. "I thought that was the worst fate in the world. I would have rather died, than to be in that situation. But I was wrong. This is worse.

"What would I do if you—?"

My diversion hadn't swayed him for a moment. "It wasn't me. It was Wyatt. And I'm OK." I put my hand on his cheek, wanting to comfort him but knowing I couldn't make the pain go away.

"I know, but it could have been you. It could have been any of us." He held me again and whispered, "We have to find out why they're still watching us and what they're planning. We have to find out what happened to Wyatt. We have to—" He had begun to hyperventilate, and I could hear his heart racing in his chest.

"M, Merick!" At the sound of his name on my lips he turned, his breathing returning to normal. "It's OK, M. We will do all those things, I promise. But first..."

First what? What are we, two powerless sector residents just out of Selection Week, supposed to do? I wondered.

"...first we need to get some rest. OK? We'll deal with this in the morning. There isn't anything we can do tonight, not with the hunt already started. Besides, whoever sent me this photo probably just wanted to scare me. I'm not going to let them. OK?"

"Yeah, yeah OK."

"Besides, if my suspicions are right, I'm pretty sure I know who it was," I said.

"Who?"

"N. Nash. I already know he was watching us the night we…"

"Our first kiss."

"Yeah. So it makes sense that this would have been him too."

"Let's not think about that tonight. We can deal with him later." Merick's heartrate was back to normal and the color had returned to his cheeks. He leaned back against the wall and wrapped his arms around me. Heat radiated off his chest and arms, surrounding me in a warm cocoon of comfort. It didn't take long for me to drift off to sleep.

6

He probably shouldn't have, it is against the rules after all, but Merick stayed the night. When I woke up some time in the late evening-early morning hours we were curled up in bed, him above the sheets and me under them. His arms were still wrapped around me as if he couldn't let go, and I didn't want him to. Being wrapped in his arms and surrounded by the sweet smell of him was more comforting than I ever could have imagined. Yet, it didn't prevent the nightmares from coming when I closed my eyes and dozed off again.

The nightmares were different this time. Instead of feeling a pull toward someone searching for me, I found myself running away. I could feel the others all around me—vampires and lycanthropes—searching, hunting. Hunting me—no, not me. As I ran, searching for cover, I saw my passing reflection in the glass of a broken window—C's reflection. *They're hunting C—Ciara!* I kept running and, although I couldn't see her, I could feel her desperation, her fear. As the hunters combed the woodlands around me/her, I hid in the thickets under the trees, and buried myself in a bed of moss and dried leaves.

"C!" I woke up at three in the morning, clutching my vision stone in my left hand and gasping for breath, cold sweat dripping down my face. I didn't even remember grabbing the stone before climbing into bed. Maybe I hadn't.

Merick stirred in the bed behind me, mumbling in his sleep. "I can get her if you want." Then he drifted back to sleep, and his breathing leveled out into long deep breaths.

The details of my dream escaped me, but the feelings of fear and anxiety remained. The knowledge that C was in trouble, at least in my dream but most likely in reality as well, forced my mind awake.

It could have been just a dream—a nightmare, I told myself, but it didn't feel that way. If felt too real. I slipped out of bed, grabbed my robe from the closet door, and made my way down to the kitchen for a bottle of blood to ease the burning that was building in my throat.

I made my way to the couch, downed the blood, sat back with my eyes closed, and thought of C, Ciara. I imagined we were still selection students, sitting on my bunk in the barracks, laughing and sharing secrets. Then, I opened my eyes—her eyes— and I was there, seated in that quiet, dark room I had seen in my previous vision. I looked around and saw the same sterile walls, empty shelves, and barren closet with the doors hanging off the hinges.

"C?" I whispered, trying not to startle her this time.

She scanned the room. "A?" She was out of breath, as if she had been running, and sounded scared, but not scared of me—not this time.

63

"Ciara, where are you?"

"I can't. It's not safe for you." She was whispering, but I didn't understand why. From what I could tell she was alone.

Ciara, listen to me. Don't talk, whatever you're thinking—I'll hear. Don't worry about anyone else eavesdropping.

"What do you mean...?"

Shhh. You don't have to say it out loud. I'm not really there, but you can still talk to me. OK?

"But I don't understand." She was standing now, I could feel her moving through the room. At first her erratic, almost frantic movements made me feel lightheaded and nauseous. Then she stopped and I saw it—her reflection in a dusty old mirror hanging on the far wall. The image was distorted and broken with the cracks in the glass, but it was her—Ciara—C.

Ciara, I need you to go to the mirror. She did as I asked. *Can you wipe the dust off the mirror?* Again, she did exactly what I asked without questioning me. The left side of her face was covered in bruises and her once vibrant red hair was brown from the dirt and tangled through with leaves and sticks. Her clothes were torn and covered with mud...and blood.

I couldn't help but wonder what had happened to her. This was not the Ciara I had known all my life. She had always been so full of life, and confidence. Ciara had known from the day she was born exactly what she wanted in life, and how to get it. I had always admired that about her, but this... I couldn't imagine what had happened to her to bring her to where she was now.

What happened to you, C?

"I..."

I/she swallowed hard, and the movement felt foreign to me, in her body. I tried to move, but she was resisting me. I didn't want to push her too hard. *It's OK, you don't have to tell me, not yet. Can you go to the window?*

"I...I can't."

Yes you can. Go to the window—please. I need to see what's out there. She didn't move, and I could feel the panic start to rise inside of her. *C, you need to trust me right now. All I want to do is help you, but I can't do that unless you tell me...show me...where you are.*

It took a few minutes, but she finally did as I asked. I probably could have forced her to go to the window, but she was already afraid, and I didn't want to scare her even more. When she looked outside, it was dark; even the street lights were out. *That's strange,* I thought to myself. *The street lights never turn off at night.* She appeared to be a few stories up, and looking down to the street I could see a long stretch of road, but no other buildings around. In the distance, I saw smoke and fire coming out of what seemed to be a large trash bin. Nothing I saw made sense.

Right C, that's excellent. Now, do you remember how you got here? Maybe C would be able to help me make sense out of what I was seeing.

"I...I don't know. I just kept running. I was so afraid. I...I didn't know what else to do." She was shaking, and I could feel her start pulling away.

"No! C, stay with me."

65

"A, it isn't safe for you here. You can't come back, or they'll think you were involved."

"Involved? Involved in what?"

"They'll think you helped me." She was whispering again, but her words seemed to scream their way through my mind.

Wait...what? What did she just say? I thought to myself, but she heard me.

"I never meant to hurt him, A."

C, what do you mean? Hurt who? Who will they think I helped you hurt?

"I didn't mean to A. I didn't mean to. I swear by the stars above, I didn't mean to hurt him. I...I loved him." She ran back to the bed and curled into a ball in the corner. I could feel the tears welling up in my/her eyes, and the cold wetness as they started to stream down our cheeks. "Promise me. Promise me you won't tell anyone."

"I..." I wanted to make that promise, I swear I did, but something was stopping me. Something was pulling me away. "C, did you kill him? Did you kill Wyatt?"

She didn't answer, and just at that moment a loud crashing sound came from somewhere beyond the bedroom door. She screamed, and suddenly I was being pushed out of her mind. "No, C, don't go!" I cried out, but it was no use; she wasn't going to let me back in. When I opened my eyes, I was back in Iris's living room, sitting in the dark.

"Is there something you want to tell me?" Iris asked, from somewhere behind me.

I jumped off the couch, scrambling to my feet. "I...um...what did you hear?"

"I'm not sure." She was standing against the wall, almost cloaked by the shadows, but it wasn't the same as when a vampire uses the shadows for protection. Vampires have the ability to become almost invisible to others by bending and weaving shadows around themselves. It's a cool trick, one I hope to learn someday. "Were you talking to Ciara? Is she here?" Iris slowly made her way toward the couch, checking the room as she moved.

"No, she's not here."

"Then how?" She stood in front of the couch, staring down at me.

"I don't know what you mean, I wasn't talking to anyone. It was just a dream. That's all." I stood up, hoping to put an end to the conversation, but it didn't work.

Iris sat down in a chair across from where I now stood. "It wasn't a dream," she said, as I squirmed under her gaze. "You have to learn to trust me Zelina. If you don't, I can't help you...or Ciara."

Trust you? You had me tied to a chair for over sixteen hours, and I hadn't done anything wrong. How can I trust you not to hurt Ciara?

"I'm trying, but how do I know you won't just hurt her?"

"I give you my word," she said, as if that was supposed to reassure me. She paused before continuing. "You're right. I'm sorry. You shouldn't trust me, not with your secrets, not if I'm unwilling to share my own." She gestured me back onto the couch across from her. "Please, sit with me."

I sat down, but I told myself it was because I was tired, and not because she wanted me to. I never took my eyes off of her, determined to maintain some semblance of control.

Iris stared at her feet as she fiddled with her hands, a nervous habit she'd had ever since I was young, and probably long before that. "I have been a Council member for over sixty years. I was one of the first."

Exactly my point! I rolled my eyes.

"Please, let me finish."

Wait, did she hear that? I watched her for a reaction, but there was none. She just continued.

"The sectors were set up to protect our members. No, they aren't perfect, and many of them have been closed because they proved to be more harmful than helpful. However, Sector C is still thriving. We don't always work well together, the lycanthropes and the vampires, but we try. I know the Council has its problems, but there are a few of us who see the potential for change, and we are working to make those changes. It isn't an easy road, and much of it must be done in secrecy, which can be difficult. But I believe, as do the others, that you…you are the answer we've been waiting for." She moved to sit next to me on the couch, and grabbed my hand.

"You have the gifts we've been looking for," Iris said. "Every year a new selection class makes it through the program. Some students go on to be excellent additions to the sector; others leave— abandoning the sector and their friends to join the castaways in the wastelands. But until you came along there hasn't been a single student to show the potential, the talent, and the strength that you have. Not to mention the fact that your body proved to be capable of not only surviving the effects of contracting both vampirism and lycanthropy but actually thriving because of it."

"Wait, you mean there have been others?"

"Over the years, yes. But…none of them ever survived."

"What are you saying? You did this to me on purpose? Why?"

"No, not on purpose. We hadn't intended to test this year. It has been a few years since our last test, and we had planned to wait another year or two. Then, when Merick infected you…"

"You mean with his partial transformation?"

"We're not sure that's what it was," Iris quickly corrected me. "His 'infecting' you was an accident. We're still not sure how he was able to shift outside of the moon cycle. But when he did, your body didn't react in the same way that all the others had. We thought then that you might be different. We chose to test you by injecting you with the lycanthropy virus of a lion to see how your body would respond—to see if both viruses could bond with the vampire virus that had already begun to alter your cellular structure."

"My cellular structure?"

"Your genetic material, yes."

"So I was just a test subject! Nice."

"No, you don't understand. You're so much more than that. When you survived the wolf infection, we had our proof that both viruses could live, concurrently, inside one host. You are not only a full-blooded vampire, you are also a lycanthrope!"

"We don't know that yet!" I corrected her.

"Yes, we do. It doesn't matter if you're able to change form or not, you still have the blood of a lycanthrope flowing through your veins. That alone makes you part of both worlds."

What was I supposed to say to that? She was right, I could feel it in my bones, and yet I had no idea what it really meant.

"Work with me. Help me. If you do that, then I can help you too." She was pleading and yet, *why? What could I possibly do for her?*

"Help you what?"

"Help me stop the war. Help me eliminate the Governing Council."

I was off the couch and across the room faster than I knew I could move. "Eliminate the Council! Are you crazy?"

"Once we eliminate the Governing Council it will be easier to dissolve the Sector Council. People will be scared at first—they won't understand—but with time things will change, and vampires and lycanthropes will be forced to coexist."

"Have you lost your mind?"

We must have been a little louder than I thought because even before I heard Merick making his way down the stairs and through the kitchen, I could smell him. That thick sweet scent washed over me as he came into the room. "What's going on in here? A, are you OK?"

"No, no I don't think I am." I hadn't turned to see him come in. I hadn't taken my eyes off of Iris.

Then I did look. "A, what's going on?" He was standing there, in the doorway between the kitchen and the living room, wearing only his tee-shirt and boxer shorts.

Oh my stars. When did he get undressed?

"A, what's going on?"

I fainted.

7

"A. A, wake up." I opened my eyes, and the sun was shining brightly through the front window. Merick was sitting next to me on the couch, lifting my hair back off of my face. "Good morning beautiful."

"Hey."

"Hey, yourself." He smiled.

"You're still here."

"Of course I'm here. Did you think I wouldn't be?"

"No. I don't know. Maybe." I looked around but didn't see Iris anywhere. "Did Iris freak out when she realized you stayed the night?"

"She wasn't happy, but no, she didn't freak out."

"Do you think she will...?"

"Tell the Council? No, I don't believe so. I'm pretty sure she doesn't support the whole 'no contact with other sector members unless you're in a family unit,' policy. I don't think she's drunk the kool-aid in that regard."

"Drunk the kool-aid?" I had no idea what he was talking about.

"It's a figure of speech. Earnest used to say it all the time. It means to believe something so strongly that you can't see any other option or perspective. It also has something to do with blindly following a leader, to the point of unreasonable behaviors."

"What kind of unreasonable behaviors?"

"You know, doing things no sane person would do, like killing people, or themselves. He said there was something in the history books about a man, Jimmy or Jim something, who had a bunch of followers. He convinced them all to drink poisoned kool-aid. They did it because they believed he knew what was best for them. In the end, it was a mass suicide."

"Oh." I had never heard the phrase before, but I guess it made sense. "So what is kool-aid?"

"He said it's kind of like juice, but it doesn't come from fruit; it comes from sugar."

I thought about that for a while. The idea of drinking sugar didn't sound all that appealing, but then again we drink water, mostly. We also get milk from the cows here in Sector C, and on rare occasions fruit juice is shipped in from one of the other sectors.

"What time is it?" I asked.

"Seven, and you stood me up for the second day in a row." He was fighting a grin that crept onto his face.

"Stood you up?"

"Yeah, you were supposed to meet me out on the course yesterday morning. Granted, you were tied up all night, but, still, I figured you'd make it up this morning."

"Oh, I—"

"I'm kidding, A. You barely got any sleep last night. Besides, I didn't wake up until about forty-five minutes ago either."

"Forty-five minutes—? But you—"

"I fell back asleep after you passed out. Iris said you probably needed the rest. So I took advantage of it. After I explained why I was still here, I lay down here on the couch with you."

"She said I needed the rest?" Clipped scenes—images, memories—of my late night conversation with Iris flashed through my mind. The fear of what she might do to Ciara propelled me off the couch. "Is she here? Is she upstairs?"

"No, she left after you passed out. That was a few hours ago. I haven't seen her since. Why? What's wrong?"

"Nothing. I mean, I don't know. She..." *She what?* I thought. What could I really say to make him understand?

He stood up and sat me back down on the couch, then turned to the table behind him and grabbed a tray. "Breakfast?"

NO, I DON'T WANT BREAKFAST! I screamed in my head. Then I smelled it and my mouth started to water.

There was a glass of warm blood, a bowl of what looked like grits, a stack of toast, and a plate of— "Steak? For breakfast?"

"Um, yeah. Lycanthropes need the protein." He cut a piece of steak, and held it out to me.

"But I'm not—"

"Yes, you are. Eat it. The protein will do you some good, and then when you've finished we'll go to work."

"Work?" *I can't go to work, not with everything else going on.*

"You didn't think you'd get out of your liaison duties that easily did you?"

"M, I can't go to work. There's a hunt going on, and I have a bad feeling that—" I stopped myself; I wasn't ready to tell him that C might have been the one who killed Wyatt. I couldn't live with myself if I was wrong and they captured her anyway.

"You can't help with the hunt, at least not from out there. They'll find whoever killed Wyatt, but until they do, we can take advantage of the surveillance feeds at the Council offices and see what we can find out on our own."

"But—"

"No, no arguing." He put the fork up to my mouth and the steak practically melted right there on my tongue.

I'm not sure how much of the steak I actually tasted, but every bite was gone, along with the glass of blood and the toast. I didn't touch the grits. I have never been a fan of grits, and I'm guessing that turning into a lycanthrope wasn't going to change that.

"Feeling better?"

"Actually, yes." And surprisingly enough it was true.

"Good. Now, go upstairs, shower, and get ready. We have to leave in thirty minutes or we'll be late." He smiled, then made his way into the kitchen with the tray and the dishes.

Oh, that smile.

After I had regained my composure, I went back up to my room and pulled out some clean clothes for the day. The shower felt amazing on my sore muscles. I hadn't even realized how sore I really was. I guess being tied up for so long had done more to me than I had realized.

8

Merick and I went our separate ways once we got to the Council building. M went in through the back, to the Lycanthrope Council offices, and I made my way to the front entrance, where the Vampire Council offices were located.

"Good morning, Calliope." I smiled as I approached Remy's assistant, who sat at her desk just outside his office. Calliope, in an effort to hide a long thin scar that ran down the left side of her face, always wore her hair down. Today was no different.

She looked a little surprised to see me, but she hid it well, and she smiled, nonetheless. "Good morning, Zelina. Do you need me to show you the way to the liaison office?" She started to stand but quickly sat back down, looking almost relieved, when I shook my head.

"No, I think I can find my way. First, though, if possible, I'd like to talk to Councilman Remy. Is he in his office?" I gave her my sweetest smile, taking a lesson from *The Book of O*. "Kill them with kindness," O154 always said. I wondered for a moment if she still felt that way. O, now Opal, had been assigned as a breeder after Selection Week. No one was more surprised than she was but, honestly, the more I think about it, the less it surprises me.

'No, I'm sorry, he's out right now. He won't be back this morning; he had a meeting that—"

Just then, Councilman Remy walked out of his office as if on cue, and much to Calliope's distaste. "Calliope, please hold my calls this—. Zelina, what a surprise. How are you feeling this morning? I'm surprised you made it in today."

I looked back at Calliope, who was redder in the face than I think I've ever seen a vampire look. It was almost as if the life had literally been poured back into her.

"I'm all right," I said. "A little tired, but I needed the distraction."

"Distraction?" He was eyeing me up and down as if sizing up an opponent.

"From Iris's apartment. I was just feeling a little claustrophobic, that's all. I hope it's all right that I came in."

"Always." He smiled, but it wasn't a happy smile. It didn't reach his eyes. We stood there in silence for what felt like forever but was probably only seconds before he filled the void. "Was there something you needed?"

"Well, only if you're not too busy. Calliope said you were out, at a meeting." I could feel the elderly vampire's eyes burning a hole into my neck, but I didn't bother to turn and look at her. "She said you wouldn't be back this morning. But since you *are* here, would you maybe have a couple of minutes to spare?"

"Of course. Please, come in. Have a seat, I'll be right with you." He held the door open for me but didn't follow me in right away. I sat down in one of the big leather seats in front of his desk, and waited. The office didn't seem as overwhelming as it had the first time I was there. Or maybe I was just not as easily intimidated as I had been a few days ago.

As I looked around, I noticed something interesting. *There aren't any flashing lights. No cameras. Hmm,* I thought to myself. Seeing the familiar blinking red light of the surveillance cameras conveniently located throughout the sector becomes second nature: you don't even notice them unless, it seems, they are absent. I made a mental note. I wasn't sure how, but I figured that little bit of knowledge just might come in handy later on.

I could hear Remy and Calliope talking in hushed whispers, but I couldn't make out what they were saying. Straining to hear, I only caught bits and pieces of their conversation. "I would have told you, but…" "…no matter, she's here now." "Contact the others and tell them not to come just yet. I'll call when I'm ready." It wasn't enough to put together any real information.

The door opened, and I quickly turned back around, toward the window, and stared out at the people passing by on their way to work, or back to their homes. "You wanted to see me?" Remy asked as he made his way back to his desk. He sat down in the chair next to mine instead of taking his seat across the desk from me. Maybe he meant it as a friendly gesture, but I was more inclined to think he meant it as an intimidation technique. Iris had said that there were others on the Council, and throughout the sector, who believed as she did—that I was the solution—but she hadn't said who. I wasn't sure I could trust Remy just yet, and erring on the side of caution seemed to be a good idea.

"I did. I wanted to talk to you about what happened yesterday."

His small, beady, blue eyes narrowed as he glared at me. "Yes, about that, I am very sorry."

No, you're not, I thought, but I didn't dare say it out loud.

"I'm not here for your apologies, sir. I know that the Council was only doing what they felt was right. Besides, I'm sure, with your job, you have to make a lot of hard decisions." I waited, watching his eyes. His pupils, as I suspected, flashed. It was only for a second, but in that second I saw rage, anger, and something else—concern? Maybe.

"Then, what is it that you want?"

Yes, it was definitely concern.

"I want to help." That got his attention. "Wyatt was a friend of mine, or as close to friends as selection students can be. We grew up together, and if someone actually did kill him then I want to help find them." I already had my suspicions about who had killed Wyatt, and the last thing I wanted was to turn C in to the Council. However, if I was going to find her— *protect* her—I was going to need their resources, and if that meant pretending to help them, so be it.

"Oh. Well I appreciate the sentiment, I do think it's best if we leave that matter up to the security teams."

Exactly what I was hoping he would say.

He stood up as if he was ready to dismiss me, but I didn't give him the chance.

"I understand. I had to try though, right?" I continued my little act.

"Of course."

"I mean I am the Council liaison, right?"

"You are." His voice was hesitant, as if he suspected that I was luring him into a trap.

"As the liaison, I have access to sector residents who might be—how should I put it—more receptive to talking with me, than with sector security?" The idea was to get him to let me interview residents, to see if anyone had seen anything. Of course, I would use this information to my own advantage. If I could get to C before sector security could, then maybe I could protect her.

"I suppose that in an ideal world that would be true. However, Zelina, you must understand that most of the residents here in Sector C are still...how should I put this?" He sat back down and reached out and took my hand. His cold hand around mine was unnerving. "Well, they are still unsure as to your role in our society."

My role? I thought. That wasn't at all what I had expected him to say.

"Most residents aren't as understanding as the Council and myself."

I couldn't help but grumble at the idea that the Council was *understanding* in any way, let alone of me and my situation. It was actually laughable, but at least I was able to contain my laughter.

"We knew that putting you in this position wouldn't be easy. It's going to take time for our residents to get used to you and comfortable with the idea of what you represent—the hope..." He went silent, and stared vacantly at the window.

"In that case," *I need a new plan...I need a new scheme...* "If I can't be of any help with the hunt, then maybe it would be best if I..." *If I what?* I wondered. "If I ...rest. I have been feeling unusually tired lately, and my muscles seem to ache more than I'm used to. It's almost as if..." *Almost as if I were still a selection student and just finished a fight,* I thought, but that wasn't it. All of a sudden I knew—I was changing—my body was changing. The realization of what that might mean, if it really was the beasts within me, struck me like a shock to my system.

"As if?" Again he was watching me—studying me—as if he wasn't sure if he should be on guard and prepared to react, should I make any sudden moves, or if something exciting was about to happen.

"As if I'm getting sick, but I'm sure it's nothing." I smiled, swallowing back my fear. "However, I don't want to get behind in my work. If it's all right with you, I'd like to take some of the sector files back to Iris's apartment with me. I'd like to study while I'm there resting, it will help with the boredom, if that's all right."

"You mean out of the office?"

"If it's all right with you of course. I was just thinking, what with the moon cycle starting in a few days, it might be better if I'm not in the office right now."

"I don't know, I'm not sure that's a good idea." Just then the phone on his desk rang and he reached to grab it, never taking his eyes off me. "Please, excuse me for just a moment."

I crossed to the wet bar on the other side of his office and pulled a bottle of blood from the mini refrigerator. I needed something to keep me calm. *Just stay calm, just stay calm.* Lifting the bottle to my lips the scent washed over me, and I was suddenly aware of how hungry I really was. Although I had eaten a rather large breakfast, it hadn't completely taken my hunger away.

"A breach? When?" Remy asked into the phone. "Did you check with the clinic? Are you sure it wasn't just another...?" I stood there listening, and the sound of his voice changed from annoyance to anger. "Then why wasn't I informed last night when it happened?"

Last night?

I fought the urge to turn and watch him, but I could feel his anger growing—filling the room. "What do you mean you just found out? Never mind, it doesn't matter. I want them found! Do you understand?" He slammed the phone down onto the desk and was gone before I could take my first sip.

I walked out of the office, bottle in hand, and Calliope was sitting at her desk, open-mouthed, staring at the computer screen. I leaned in to see what she was reading and saw a memo titled "Population Update." The only thing else on the screen was the number 35,758.

"35,758? That's three in two days."

She quickly turned off the screen with a swipe of her hand across the front of the monitor. "I'm sorry, Zelina, Councilman Remy had to step away for a bit."

I could hear the silent knocking of opportunity, and I decided to open the door. "No worries. He actually already helped me with everything I needed. I'm gonna stop by the liaison office to pick up a few things, and then he said I could take the next few days off, just through the moon cycle of course."

"Of course," she said, smiling.

As I walked away, I heard her dialing the phone. I turned the corner, leaned against the wall, and concentrated on her soft, sweet voice.

"I'm sorry to bother you, sir. Yes, I know. Yes sir, I understand, but this is urgent too. It's about Zelina." There was a long pause as she tapped her fingers on the desk in front of her. The sound thump-thump-thumped like a rhythm in my head.

"What is it now?" Remy sounded angry, or maybe just annoyed. I quickly looked around, but he wasn't there. I realized he wasn't talking to me, he was talking to Calliope, on the phone, and I was overhearing, as if I were Calliope.

"I just wanted you to know she will be taking a few days off," Calliope said. "She has requested—" I could feel—sense—that she was about to bring up the files and I quickly silenced her, pushing her out of her own mind.

"Yes, I know that already," Remy said. "Just make sure she doesn't remove any of the Council regulations from the office."

"Of course sir. Sorry to bother you," I/she answered before hanging up the phone. I quickly pulled out of her mind, leaving room for her to re-enter, hoping that she wouldn't have noticed. I listened for a while longer, but she just went right back to her typing. I took a deep breath; I was in the clear, and I continued down the hall.

I banged on the large metal door that led to the liaison office, and William looked down at me through the window. "Oh, Zelina! We didn't expect to see you this morning." William is a large man, bigger than any other vampire I had ever seen, and bigger than most lycanthropes too. He has blue-black hair with a hint of gray at the temples, and sky blue eyes. The long scar that ran down the left side of his face, although gruesome, somehow made him more approachable and even a little alluring.

"You have the same scar," I said, remembering the scar that mirrored his, on Calliope's left cheek.

"Excuse me?"

"Nothing. I…" *Crap.* "You thought you would only be watching me at night for a while, right?" I asked with a smile, but he didn't say anything. "So, do I get to come in, or are you just going to watch me from there?"

He stepped back, and I could hear him fumbling with the lock before be pulled the large door open. "Sorry about that."

"Oh, William, you know better than that. There is no need for an apology." Apologies are seen as a sign of weakness in Sector C, and especially among the vampires. "Besides, you didn't know that I already knew that you and Haden—good morning, Haden—had been assigned to be my own personal security guards; or, should I say, watch dogs?" They shared a quick glance of uncertainty. It was written all over their faces; they had no idea whether they should respond or just keep quiet in case I didn't know everything.

I just laughed.

After opening the door to my office, *my office—* the thought brought a small smile to my face—I looked back over my shoulder at Haden and William, who were quietly sitting at their posts. "I won't be long. I just need to grab a few things. Not sure what your plans are, if you're supposed to just watch me during the day or if you've already been assigned to night duty, but if you're coming with me when I leave, you might want to pack up." Then I was gone, safe and secure behind closed doors, at least for now.

9

"Where have you been?" Merick asked as the door shut behind me. "I was worried."

"What do you mean?" I looked down at my monitor: eight twenty-two. *Hmmm, that took me a little longer than I thought.* "I stopped by Councilman Remy's office before coming here."

He was at my side, grabbing my arm before I even saw him leave his seat. "You did what?"

"How did you do that?" I didn't pull away exactly, but he had startled me enough that I wasn't sure what to do. "How did you get over here so fast? Did you teleport?"

He just laughed and smiled down at me. "Teleport? Are you kidding? That's not even a thing, except in old movies." I almost laughed. I had seen firsthand that teleporting was, in fact, a real thing, but, before I had a chance to correct him, he interrupted my thought. "I'm a wolf, baby! I've got all sorts of tricks up my sleeve." Then he pulled me closer, and leaned in. "I'm glad you're OK," he whispered, and kissed me. It was soft and sweet—until it wasn't.

My body reacted to his touch. Without my brain telling it what to do, and before I could think to stop it, my arms were wrapped around his waist and my hands were pulling the back of his shirt out of his pants. His hands held my hips tight against his, and I could feel his strength as he tried to pull me even closer. His skin burned under my fingers, the heat radiated off of him, and I could feel droplets of perspiration on my own forehead and around my neck.

"Grrr..." It was an intense rumble, a growl, coming from deep in Merick's throat.

I responded with a groan, or moan, of my own.

I ran my hands along his back, and he mirrored my movements with his own hands. I hadn't even noticed we had moved across the room until we somehow landed on the couch, his weight pushing me down into the soft cushions of the sofa. I'm not sure how far I would have let it go—if I would have been able to stop it—if Haden hadn't started banging on the door.

"Just a second," Merick called. He jumped off of the couch to answer the door as I ran to my desk, adjusting my clothes and fixing my hair on the way. "What." When he yanked open the door, Haden and William rushed in with their guns up and at the ready. "Woo, wait. What's going on?"

In seconds, Haden had Merick slammed against the wall, and William was at my side with his hand firmly on my shoulder as he scanned the room. "The office is secure," William announced.

"Uh, of course it is. It's only the two of us in here. You're the only ones with the keys. Wouldn't you know if you had let anyone else in?" Merick said sarcastically as he tried, unsuccessfully, to push his way out of Haden's grip.

As I started to stand, William released my shoulder and reached down to help me up. "No thanks, I got it." I stood up and started crossing toward Merick. "Mind letting him go?"

"Sorry ma'am, can't do that."

"You can't or you won't?" I asked.

"Is there really a difference?" Haden answered.

I looked back at William, who, as I suspected, was following close behind. "There is to me. If you can't, it means someone told you to secure him. If you won't, it means you're acting on your own. So which is it?"

"I..." He looked back at William, who nodded. "I can't ma'am."

"Stop calling me that! I'm not a ma'am, I'm only seventeen." I reached out to Merick, unsure how Haden would react. "M, come here." Much to my surprise, Haden let him go. Merick quickly grabbed my hand and stood by my side—a united front. I always felt stronger—safer—with M next to me.

"What is going on?" Merick asked, but neither Haden nor William answered him.

"No sir, they're both here..."

I turned around, thinking that maybe William was talking to himself. "Who are you—?"

Haden quickly clasped his hand over my mouth, "Shhh. Don't interrupt."

"...Yes, sir. OK, we'll move forward as planned." With that, he looked back at Merick and me. "Sorry for the interruption. If you need anything, we'll be just outside." They turned to leave without another word.

"Excuse me?" The door shut and they never even looked back. "What was that?" Merick asked to no one.

"That was life as we know it: changing."

"What?"

"I don't know, never mind me."

"Are you OK?"

"Yeah, I'm fine," I answered, but I really wasn't. "Did you hear?"

"Hear what?"

I glanced back toward the door because I knew Haden and William would be listening, then motioned for Merick to follow me back to my desk. "There's been a sector breach, and apparently the population count dropped again last night."

His mouth dropped open, and his voice was little more than a whisper when he answered. "Seriously?"

The last five minutes replayed in my mind over and over. I couldn't help feeling that I had somehow missed something, but I didn't know what. "Listen, I think I'm gonna head back to Iris's place."

"You're leaving? Now?"

"Yeah, I already got it approved this morning. I'm taking the next few days off. What with the moon cycle starting soon, and the fact that I'm not sure if I'll be human or if my beasts are planning to take over, I think I'm going to need a nap. Besides, my muscles are aching and I'm feeling really drained."

"Your beasts? Been talking to Iris, have you?"

He was smiling. After everything that had just happened, he was smiling. "I have."

"Well, if you get some time off, I think it's only fair that I do too. Besides, it will be my first moon cycle too, you know. The first time my wolf gets to come out and play. Maybe I should head over to Iris's place to rest, too."

I was sorting the files on my desk into two piles—take, and leave—when I felt my cheeks flush. "I'm not sure we would get much rest if we both went to her place," I ventured, hesitantly. "Besides, I also have some reading to do." I held up the thick stack of papers to show him the extent of my homework.

"You can't take those you know."

"Actually, I can. Remy approved it this morning." Yeah, approved was maybe stretching it a bit, but what Remy didn't know wouldn't hurt him. "OK, he didn't necessarily agree to it, but he didn't flat out say no either."

"Yeah, I don't think that's the same thing, A. What if those guys"—he nodded toward the door— "were coming in here to make sure you hadn't taken the files?"

"If that were the case they wouldn't have just left. They would have—" I was going to say they wouldn't have left without searching my desk, but I stopped myself and quickly began searching through the stack of files again. *Resident Housing Assignments, Student Housing Assignments, Town Hall Meetings, Resident Activities, Sector Student Activities, External Security Measures, Breeder Selection, Sector Position Assignment, Dining Facility Regulations, etc., etc., etc. It's gone.* "It's gone!" I cried.

"What's gone?"

"The file on internal security measures." I looked up, meeting Merick's gaze. "Serenity's security regulations."

Lucky for me, Haden and William hadn't thought to search Merick's desk. "Can I see yours?"

"Seriously?" he asked for the second time in as many minutes.

"Yes, seriously. If that's the only file they took it must be the one Councilman Remy doesn't want me reading. That means it's the only one I actually need." He lifted the file off his desk and brought it to me.

"If you get my file, what do I get?"

I tilted my head back, pulled him closer, and gazed into his beautiful eyes. "A kiss?"

"Fair enough." He leaned down and kissed me.

"Oh, hey, wait a second." I pulled out of his arms.

"What? What's wrong?"

"No, nothing. I just…have you seen any maps anywhere?"

"Um…" He crossed to the bookshelves along the wall to the left of the door. I hadn't even taken the time to look at the bookshelves, let alone figure out what was on them. "I think I saw some old sector maps yesterday. Some of them even showed parts of the wastelands." As he continued to look, I went back to my desk to sift through the files I hadn't yet read. I needed to figure out who Ciara's mentor was and where she had been assigned to live. If I could figure that out, maybe I could find her.

"Why do you need them?"

M interrupted my thoughts. "What?"

"The maps, why do you need the maps?"

"I just do," I snapped. "I'm sorry. I...I didn't mean it like that. It's just that I have an idea about who might have—you know."

"Wyatt?"

"Yeah, but..." I glanced up at the familiar blinking light in the corner. "...I don't think we should talk about it here, but maybe tonight?"

"The course?" Of course he would suggest meeting out at the selection course—it's our spot. It's where we became an *us* for the first time, even if we weren't—or *aren't*—ready to admit it.

"Yeah. Seven?"

"OK." He handed me a few folded maps; they were old and faded, but they were the best we had. "A?"

"Yeah?"

"Don't get caught with these, OK?"

"I won't, I promise." I kissed him one more time, then shoved the maps and files under my jacket, and headed for the door.

'Be safe.' He didn't say it, not out loud, but his voice and his thought were there in my mind just the same. I looked back, nodded, and was out the door.

10

William and Haden escorted me to Iris's apartment, and when we got there the door was already open. I didn't hear anyone talking inside. "Iris?" I pushed the door the rest of the way open. "Are you home?" She didn't respond.

"Let us search the premises before you enter," William said, pushing past me.

"I don't think that's necessary," I said. I was about to tell him that I couldn't smell anyone or hear any other heartbeats inside, but it was too late. He and Haden were already inside, making their way through the apartment, room by room.

I must have forgotten to shut it this morning, I thought to myself. Although, I didn't really believe that.

I followed them in and locked the door behind me. I grabbed a bottle of blood and a few bags of beef jerky from the refrigerator on my way up to my room. When I got to the top of the stairs, Haden and William were just coming out of my bedroom door. "It's all clear," William announced.

"I figured as much. I didn't hear you attacking anyone up here, so…" I looked around as the three of us stood in close quarters in the narrow hallway. "So are you staying or what?"

They exchanged looks, and William nodded before Haden pushed past me and made his way down the stairs. "We're only here for your protection. You know that, right?" William asked.

"Yeah, OK." I swallowed the laughter that was bubbling up at the back of my throat. "You're here because the Council, namely Remy, assigned you to watch over me—babysit me. You're here because they're afraid of what I am or what I might turn into once the moon cycle starts. But that's not going to happen for a few days. So why are you here now?"

He opened his mouth to object, answer, explain, I'm not sure which, but I guess he thought better of it because he quickly closed it again before nodding and making his way past me to follow Haden down the stairs. "We'll wait in the hallway for Iris to arrive. Good night, Zelina."

"Good night, William." I waited, listening for the front door to shut behind the two of them and the lock to click into place. I thought about going down to lock the deadbolt as an added protection, but figured either William or Haden or both could probably break the door down anyway. A second lock wouldn't really matter.

By the time Iris made it home six hours later, I had gone through all the files and all the maps. I have to admit, even though it is tedious, I'm glad the Council ensures such thorough record-keeping, because I was able to figure out that, unlike me, Ciara and the rest of the vampire initiates had been assigned living quarters at the community center in the vampire quarters. They had been placed in the care of two vampire "counselors," who were assigned to help them get through their initial transformations and blood lust.

Why not me? I wondered, but it didn't take me long to realize that I'm not like the other vampires. Of course they wouldn't put me in the same living space as all the others.

My plan was to go over to the community center first thing in the morning to talk to the counselors. If Ciara was still there, then, at the very least, the quality of her living quarters needed to be addressed. If she wasn't there, then maybe they could give me an idea of when she had left and where she might have gone.

I had read through the sector's internal security regulations at least fifteen times, and my floor was littered with maps, but the only thing I had determined was that if C wasn't at the community center then she wasn't in Sector C. Nothing on the maps of the areas within the sector walls resembled what I had seen through her eyes. I plotted out what I thought would have been the three easiest ways out of the sector if you started from the community center. Based on that, I identified the two most likely locations for C to be hiding just beyond the wall. I wasn't really sure what my plan was beyond that. I didn't think I was crazy enough to actually try to get past the sector border patrol, but I wasn't going to leave C alone out there either.

"What are you doing?" Iris was standing at my bedroom door with her arms across her chest. I hadn't even heard her come into the apartment.

"I—nothing."

"It doesn't look like nothing to me." She picked up one of the maps. "Is this a map of the wastelands?"

"No." *Busted!* "I mean, I don't think so. I think that's just a map of—"

"Yes it is, Zelina." I could say I was saved by her interrupting me, because I actually had no idea what I had been about to say, but then again she was right. I had no explanation for why I had the maps in the first place. "What are you doing with a map of the wastelands?"

"I just..." *It's time for honesty.* "I think I know who killed Wyatt. But it was an accident. It wasn't murder. She never meant to—"

"She? She who? Ciara?"

I didn't want to answer, but I knew I had to. At some point, I was going to have to start trusting someone, and it might as well be Iris. "Yes."

"You think it was Ciara, or you know it was Ciara?" Iris looked almost as sick and upset at the idea as I felt.

"I know it was Ciara."

"Are you sure? Are you a hundred percent sure? Because if you're not sure..." She slid down the doorframe and sat with her back to the wall.

"Yes. No. I mean, I'm pretty sure. But Iris, I swear, if she did do it she didn't mean to do it."

"Where is she now?"

"I don't know."

"Don't lie to me Zelina!"

"I'm not lying. I honestly don't know. That's why I have these maps. I'm trying to find her. I...I want to help her."

Iris crawled across the floor and started gathering the maps up into a pile. "You can't." Her hands were shaking and I saw a single tear escape her eye. "If she really did kill him, then she can't be helped."

"Why are you crying? You weren't even close to her."

"Wasn't I?" She looked up, and I saw the full extent of the pain, sadness, and guilt that she was trying so hard to hide. "You kids—you were my responsibility. I cared for you, looked out for you, all your lives. Now, to have one dead, another on the run, and you... I'm not even sure what you are yet."

"You said I'm the cure."

"Right. You're the cure. The cure for a war that only a handful of us seems to want to stop. Where did I go wrong?" She finished gathering up the papers and just sat slumped over with her head in her hands. "Where did I fail?"

"You didn't fail. We're not your responsibility anymore." I took the maps out of her hand, and set all but one of them on my desk. "Listen, I don't know why all of this is happening, but I do know that you're not to blame. I'm going find Ciara before she gets hunted down, and I'm going to help her, because I know that she didn't mean to kill Wyatt—if she even did kill him. And when I'm done helping her I'm going to help you. If you really believe I could be the cure for the war between the vampires and the lycanthropes, then that's what I'll be."

"How do you plan to find her with the hunt going on? There are no fewer than a hundred guards patrolling the border right now, and who knows how many they have outside the walls. If they don't find her before the moon cycle starts in two nights, they will open the hunt to all sector residents. That means every vampire and every lycanthrope will have free reign to hunt her down—inside and outside the sector. The elder residents will be out in the wastelands hunting. Believe me, if she is out there, they will find her."

"That just means I have to find her first."

"How?"

"I have an idea of where she might be."

"You just told me you didn't know—"

"I don't know..." I interrupted. "At least I'm not positive, but that doesn't mean I don't have my suspicions. If I'm right, then maybe I can get to her first."

"Zelina, please tell me you're not thinking of trying to get out to the wastelands. You can't get past the border patrol. They've doubled security on all exits because of the breach earlier today." She looked up as if it had just hit her. "It was Ciara, wasn't it?" I didn't answer, and maybe not answering was a response in itself. "Even if you did make it out, you'd never get back in."

"Don't worry, I won't need to get out." *She didn't need to know my whole plan. In fact, the less she knew, the safer she would be.*

"You mean she's still in the sector?"

I didn't answer.

I still had two hours before I had to meet Merick, but I didn't want Iris trying to stop me so I turned to leave.

"A…" Iris whispered, and I made the mistake of looking back. "You know that if I'm asked I can't keep this from them. I can't lie to the rest of the Council. They'll know."

She was right. If nothing else, Councilman Ash would know.

"Then you won't have to." A plan was already forming in the back of my mind. "William and Haden left when you got home, right?"

"They did."

"Good." I grabbed her by the arm and pulled her downstairs to the kitchen with me. A quick search of the pantry provided a length of rope. I motioned her into one of the kitchen chairs and quickly tied her up—firmly, but not punishingly. Conflicting emotions played across her face, but she understood.

"If she runs, they'll kill her." She wasn't warning me, she was preparing me—as if she already knew Ciara's fate.

"Then what are her options?" I hadn't really thought that Ciara had any other choices, but I wasn't willing to settle for the option of death.

"I don't know. If she turns herself in, they *might* show leniency."

"Right." Death, or the possibility of mercy as defined by the Council. I guess that was the best we were going to get. "If anyone comes to find you it will already be too late. You can tell them I caught you off guard—surprised you and then tied you up before you had a chance to fight."

"But that—"

Reluctantly, I shoved a dishrag into her mouth, curtailing her ability to argue. "That's exactly how it

happened. Do you understand?" She nodded. "Good."
I headed for the door but turned back before leaving.
"I'll be back. I promise."

11

Two hours later I had made it to the community center and tracked the easiest access to the border wall from there. I ran along the wall, making note of the numbers and positions of the patrol guards. I pretended to be "training," for what, I have no idea. But each of the twelve guards I passed accepted that as an excuse, and happily let me go along my way with a "Good luck!" or a "Wow, great job!" or, my personal favorite, "I bet you're gonna win!" Perhaps they just didn't recognize me with my hair pulled back and my black hooded sweatshirt covering half my face.

Two hours wasn't even remotely enough time to make it all the way around the sector—not even with my newly pumped-up vampire speed. I focused on a few key points of interest I had spotted on the map closest to where Ciara had probably exited. The rest would have to work itself out one way or another.

By the time I made it to the Selection Week obstacle course, Merick was already there waiting for me. He rushed toward me. "Why are you all red?"

"What?" *Crap!* I quickly wiped the sweat from my forehead and rearranged my ponytail. "I've been running."

"You know, you're kinda cute when your cheeks are all red and sweaty."

Oh my stars, did he just say that?

"Stop that!" I grabbed his arm and pulled him into the woods near the starting line of the course. "You know we can't be caught talking like that in public."

He stopped following me. "Yeah, but what if we could?"

"What do you mean, what if we could? That's insane. The Council would never allow..."

When I turned around, he was standing there staring down at a folded piece of paper in his hand. "Is that? Tell me that's not..." My heart was pounding in my chest, threatening to escape. In our society, all family units have to be preapproved by the Council, prior to the union being made. It's not like back in the old days when people met, dated for a while, fell in love, and got married.

The first step in getting approval for a family unit is an application that both the man and woman must sign; it is then submitted to the Council office for approval. "M, please tell me that's not an application to..."

"I..., I thought you'd be happy. I thought you felt the same..."

"I do." I took his face between my hands. *Wow, his skin is warm.* "I do. I swear by the stars above, M, I do. But you know as well as I do that they'll never let us."

Family units are only sanctioned between people of the same race or ethnicity. Vampires are only paired with vampires, wolves are only paired with wolves, lions with lions, tigers with tigers. It's been that way since the beginning of the sector. That's why we're not supposed to form any strong feelings for each other while we're selection students. Who knows how things are going to turn out after Selection Week. That's why Nash had been so devastated when Opal had been selected to be a sector breeder. Even without acting on his feelings, he had already become devoted to her, and now they would never, ever, be together.

"But A, you're more than a vampire. I keep telling you that. What if your wolf is your dominant? What if you could control—?"

"You're right, I am more than a vampire. You're right, there is a chance that come tomorrow night my wolf might find her way out. So, let's wait. Let's wait and just see what happens, OK?"

"And if she does?"

"If she does, and if we both survive the next four days, then you can ask me again."

He tucked the paper back into his pocket, safe and sound, then took a deep breath before looking back up at me. "Tell me what we have to do."

Back to business. "Not here," I said.

We walked along the trail, in silence, until we got to the warp wall. Men being what men are, M took off running as soon as the wall was in sight, and quickly vaulted to the top. "You coming?" he called.

Typical boy, always having to show off. Lucky for me, even Merick knew that I had nothing to prove.

When I reached the side of the wall, I just climbed the ladder to the top. When I got there,

Merick was rubbing his temples with his eyes closed. "You all right?" I asked, as I spread out the map.

"Yeah, I'm cool. Just a headache."

I spent the next thirty or forty minutes explaining everything. Everything.

"So she *told* you she *killed* him?" he asked, after I explained the vision I had had, or rather the conversation I had had with Ciara during my vision. It's all still so confusing, even to me.

"Yes."

"How do you know it was real, and not just a dream?"

"It's the same as when it happens with you and me. How do *you* know it's real, and not just a dream?"

"I…I'm not sure." He was just looking at me as if I had the answer that he was struggling to find. "I guess I don't? I mean, no, I don't. The first time you did it…"

"During Selection Week?"

"Yeah, during Selection Week. I guess I kinda thought I was going crazy. Hell, even after that I wasn't a hundred percent sure I wasn't just losing my mind."

"Yeah, but you weren't. So how do you explain it? Why did you listen to me that first time? Why did you tell me how to get to your room?

"My room? I…"

"What made you leave Iris's apartment the other night if you weren't sure it was me talking to you?"

He looked lost, and maybe that should have clued me in, but it didn't. "I don't know. I can't explain…"

"Exactly."

"I guess I know it's really you because it always happens when I'm wide awake?" He said it like a question, but I didn't think he expected me to answer. Then he continued, so I guess I was right. "It's not like I wake up wondering if the dream I just had actually happened, or...something else."

"Well, it wasn't a dream for me either. Besides, I'm still getting used to all this stuff, too. Teagan said that my visions are things that have either happened in the past, or are currently happening at that moment, and my premonitions are things that will happen in the future. I've never been inside the vampire living quarters within the community center, so I have no idea what condition they are in, but I do know that C has never been in a place as run-down as the room I saw her in, or at least not before now. There was only one other time..." I stopped myself, remembering the first vision—premonition—I had had of Ciara in that run-down room. It had been the night Councilman Blake had dragged me out of bed. The night they had discovered Wyatt, dead. *Had she killed him and then run? Is that run-down room the place where she had escaped to?*

"A, what are you thinking? Where did you go?" Merick said, pulling me out of my own head.

"Sorry, I was just thinking," I said. "I'm pretty sure I wouldn't have been able to communicate with her if it were somewhere in the future, so my only guess is that it's real, and that I was in the moment. These *connections*—they're just as real to me as we are, sitting here talking. I can't always control when they happen, but I'm getting better at making them happen when I need them too."

"Like when you found my room back during Selection Week."

This time it wasn't a question, but I answered him anyway. "Kinda, but sometimes it's more than just communicating. Sometimes I can actually see through the other person's eyes. I can make them talk, make them say whatever I want them to say."

"That's not—"

"Possible?"

"Yeah."

"It's possible, trust me, and I think I can use that to help Ciara."

I wasn't sure how long we had been sitting there on the warp wall, but darkness had settled in the woods around us, and slim strips of moonlight peeked through the tree branches, illuminating patches on the ground.

"So what's the plan?"

"You see here?" I had the partly-folded map spread out on my knees, and I pointed to a spot about a half mile outside of the sector wall. The map showed a symbol of a building of some kind which, being in the wastelands, would most likely be abandoned. "This is where I think she is."

"How can you be sure?"

"I can't, but it's my best guess. I've studied all the maps, and I only found two places that matched what I had seen in my vision within a mile of the sector. I figure she probably stayed close. She might be scared of getting caught, but she would be just as scared, if not more, of the castaways."

"So you're going to try to get to her? How are you—?"

"No, I don't need to get to her, not physically anyway. I just need some privacy so that I can communicate with her without Iris hearing or interrupting me again. That's where you come in."

"Me? What can I—?" His hands went again to the sides of his face. "Shit, that really hurts." When he looked back up his eyes were glossy, but he was breathing normally and seemed all right. "Sorry. I'm fine. What were you saying?"

"Are you sure?"

"Yeah, yeah I'm sure. Go on."

"See this?" I pointed to a small structure on the map just inside the sector wall, but far enough away from any of the exits that the guards probably wouldn't patrol it regularly. "I'm not sure what this building is used for, but if we can get to it I think we'll have the privacy we need." His eyes lit up when I said privacy, and I had to shake off the smile that was creeping onto my lips. "No!" I warned him. "You're not going to make me lose focus."

"What, me? I have no intentions of doing any such thing, but apparently that is where *your* mind was going." He smiled and then leaned in and kissed me before I could object.

I pulled away, reluctantly, after only a brief moment. "We're kind of on a deadline here," I said, more sternly than I really wanted to sound.

"You're right, sorry," he said, not looking at all sorry.

"Iris said that the hunt will be open to all the residents in two nights, if the killer isn't found by then.

I need—*we* need—to get to Ciara first. It's one thing trying to get her past the guards—it'll be a whole other challenge if I have to work around all the sector residents who feel inclined to join in on the hunt."

"Not to mention the fact that we'll both be locked up in the lycanthrope holding cells two nights from now, with the added comfort of Haden and William watching over us," M reminded me.

"Crap. I had forgotten about that. Do you know what time they plan to put everyone in?"

"No, but I'm sure we'll find out soon enough."

"Then we can't wait. We have to find her tonight."

"Tonight?"

"If we leave tonight, we have all night and tomorrow. I'm not sure how much time we can expect to have beyond that."

"A, they might not be expecting you at work tomorrow, but they are expecting me. What if they come looking for me?"

He was right. Remy already knew I wasn't going to be back until after the moon cycle, but there was no reason M wouldn't be at work, and if he didn't show up, it wouldn't be long before Haden and William would be hunting him down.

"You're right. I can't ask you to do this, and I'll understand if it doesn't make sense for you to come with me."

It was a crazy—*stupid*—idea, but I knew if Ciara were in my shoes, she would do whatever it took to help me. So I didn't really have another choice. I had to help her. Waiting until after the moon cycle would mean leaving her out there, being hunted, for five more nights. Who knows what kind of shape she would be in by then, if she even survived.

"What do we do with her once we get her back inside the sector walls?"

"You mean you'll come?"

"Not for Ciara, but for you I'd go anywhere."

I didn't know what to say. How do you thank someone who's about to risk their life for you?

"Now, what do we do with her once we find her?"

"I...I'm not sure."

M just stared at me. I waited for him to argue, tell me I was crazy, or just flat out refuse, but he never did. "OK," was all he said and that was enough.

12

We went our separate ways; Merick to his place to prepare and gather a few weapons he had stashed away, and me back to Iris's apartment to make sure no one had found Ciara yet. I knew it was a stupid idea, but at the very least I had to know that Iris was still there, and that no one was looking for me. If they were already tracking me, then our mission would be over before it even began.

I stood outside Iris's apartment, with my ear to the door, trying to see if I could hear any movement or heartbeats coming from inside. I had left her alone, tied to a kitchen chair and gagged. I was just hoping that she was still there, and that none of the Council members were aware of my recent absence.

Thump-thump. Thump-thump.

Her heart was racing in her chest, and she was scared. "Zelina?" She called from the other side of the door.

Crap, I thought to myself. I hadn't intended for her to realize I was there, and she must have managed to dislodge the gag.

"Zelina, I know you're there," she called again.

I decided not to stick around to see how it was going to end. She was still there, and tied up;

otherwise she would have come to the door. It was best for me just to leave.

When I got to the park where Merick and I had had our dinner picnic only a few nights ago, he was already there waiting.

I knew he was there before I even saw him. I could feel him. His heartbeat was racing and echoing all around me. Nervous? Maybe. But then I saw his face, and realized it wasn't nerves. He was excited.

"You ready for this?" I asked.

"Oh yeah." He picked up a black duffle bag from the ground at his feet, and tossed it onto the picnic table beside him. "You want some toys?" The edges of his lips were turned up in a wicked smirk that made my insides clench.

"Toys?" I stepped closer, but couldn't see into the bag. "What kind of toys?"

"Only the best kinds." He unzipped the bag, reached in, and pulled out a thin dagger, secured in a black leather sheath with a thigh strap. "This one's for you."

I took it, fastened the sheath securely around my right thigh, and then pulled out the dagger, feeling the weight of it in my hand. "It's nice. Where did you get it?"

"Let's just say, when you become a lycanthrope, stories aren't the only things the elders share with you."

"Seriously?" The only thing Britt had shared with me was her hatred.

"Seriously." His smile didn't fade as he continued to pull weapons—or toys, as he liked to call them—out of his bag.

By the time the bag was empty I had a dagger strapped to my right thigh, two spring-loaded wrist sheaths, a small folding pocket knife stuffed in my boot, a wire garrote bracelet on my left arm, and a small crossbow the size of a slingshot hanging from a corded belt around my waist. And this was nothing compared to the arsenal Merick was carrying.

"Um, M, you do know that if we do this right, we shouldn't even see any of the guards, let alone have to fight them, right?"

"Yeah," he said, "but you can't plan for the best case scenario. You have to plan for the worst case scenario and hope for the best."

When did he get so smart? I wondered.

"Besides," he continued, "you look completely badass in all-black and covered in weapons." He smirked, and then winked, before turning around. "Come on," he said, as he tossed the empty bag under the table and headed for the woods. "We're burning daylight."

I looked up at the moon, already high in the sky. "Yeah, it's already—"

"It's an expression A, just an expression." He had only gone a few feet when he stopped abruptly. I thought he must have heard something or seen someone, but then his hands flew up and gripped the sides of his own head. "What the—?"

"Are you OK?"

He slowly lowered his arms and looked back over his shoulder. He stopped when he saw me.

"M, are you OK?"

He was silent for a few seconds. It looked like he was having trouble focusing his eyes on me, but then he broke the silence, "Yeah. Yeah, I'm all right. Let's get this over with."

After about five minutes of what felt like aimless wandering I stopped to pull out the map so we could figure out where we were.

When M realized I wasn't following him anymore, he made his way back to where I was squatting under a tree. He reached down and took the small flashlight I had been aiming down at the map and switched it off. "What are you doing?"

"Isn't it obvious?"

"You don't need that." M grabbed the map, quickly folding it back up, and shoving it into his back pocket. He handed the flashlight back to me. "And this is like a beacon out here. Unless you intended to be alerting the guards that we're wandering around where we're not supposed to be."

"Yeah well, unless you've suddenly become the expert on Sector C territory and I don't know it, I think we probably do need to at least try and follow the map."

"A, tracking is kind of my thing. I've seen the map and, trust me, I know where we're going."

He said it with such confidence it was hard to argue. I had never known M to be much of a tracker. Even in class, when we had to use compasses to complete the scavenger hunts Professor Gunner set up for us, M never won. Then again, he never really tried very hard back then.

It was another thirty minutes, give or take a few, before I saw the small wooden structure in the distance. "Is that it?"

"Yeah." M stopped and crouched down, motioning for me to join him. I knelt down on the cold hard ground, feeling the heat radiating off his skin. I had to force myself not to reach out and touch his arm. I'm not sure if it was the warmth I was after or just the feel of his skin on mine. "The lights are all off, if that place even has electricity. Who knows how old it is. I think it's safe to go in, but we should probably do a perimeter check first."

"A perimeter check? What is with you? You sound like one of the guards tonight. You been hanging out with Quinn and Riker lately?" I laughed at the thought of his spending his free time with Quinn and Riker. Even when we were all classmates, he was never really close to them. They were bullies back then and they were guards now—not much had changed—but M didn't even smile.

Quinn and Riker, also known, pre-Selection Week, as Q and R, had graduated with Merick and me. They were the toughest guys in our class. Both had selected lycanthropy, and had been injected with the werebear virus. They both had been assigned positions as sector guards working under Councilman Donovan on the external sector security team. From what I had learned from Iris, werebears tend to be pretty lazy, except when working out, eating, hunting, or fighting. That pretty much described Q and R, even before Selection Week.

M never answered. "M, You been hanging out with Quinn and Riker lately?" I asked again.

M chuckled. "No." He never took his eyes from the small structure. "I'm just focused. The last thing I want is for something to happen to you. It's my job to keep you safe."

"M." I grabbed his shoulder and turned him around. There in his eyes I saw it: fear. "It is not your job to keep me safe. I brought you into this, not the other way around. If anything happens, to either of us, it will be on my shoulders, not yours. You get that, right?"

He didn't answer, just shook it off and then slowly stood up. "I'll go right. You go left. Stay at least twenty yards out at all times. When we meet up on the back side of the building we'll work our way inside. OK?"

It was his voice, but it didn't sound like him at all. "OK." I needed to give him this. He needed to be in control, to snuff the anxiety that I could see growing behind his eyes and hear in the trembling of his voice. Or maybe it wasn't anxiety. Maybe it was excitement. I prayed it wasn't excitement. Excitement causes false confidence and, in a fight, nothing can get you killed faster than false confidence.

"If you get into trouble, you call out and I'll come right to you."

"I'll be fine," I assured him. Then, watching him head off into the woods, away from me, I wondered, would *he* be OK? And if not, would *he* call out for help?

13

The building, more like a run-down cabin, was nestled deep in the woods. There were no roads or even trails leading to or from it, at least not that I had seen. I focused on the brush all around me, but didn't see any signs that anyone else had been here. There were no broken branches, bent ferns, or even disturbed ground covering. Above me, I watched for any signs of movement in the surrounding trees—nothing.

Merick was right, I couldn't see any light coming through the windows, but that didn't guarantee that no one was inside. I slid down to the ground, pulling leaves and small branches around me to shield me from any spying eyes, and low-crawled my way closer to the cabin. Once there, I held my breath, settling into my best attempt at that unearthly stillness that vampires develop over time, and listened. Silence filled the air around me. Then, startled back into reality, I heard the crunching of leaves coming from the back side of the house.

Do I go back or stay? I wondered, trying to judge the distance to the tree line, and whether or not I could make it in time. I should have been acting, not thinking.

"What are you doing?" I jumped at M's voice.

"Shit, M, you scared me." My voice was no louder than a whisper, but it didn't matter. He had crouched down and was close enough that I could feel his breath on my neck.

"Good," he hissed. "I thought I told you to stay at least twenty yards out. Are you trying to get yourself killed?" Although I thought his reaction was a bit over the top, he did have a point.

"No, I'm not trying to get myself killed. I just thought maybe I would be able to sense if there was anyone inside."

"And?"

"No. From what I can tell, we're alone." I expected to see the tension around his eyes soften, or a spark of excitement at the thought of being alone, so far out in the woods, with me, but there was nothing. No response—not even a smirk crossed his face.

"Good, then we should probably get inside before we do get seen." Merick stood and headed back the way he had come from and turned the corner behind the house without even looking back.

Once inside, Merick moved from room to room, in the small four-room cabin, checking every inch of the place to make sure we were in fact alone. "It's all clear."

"OK. Do you think we should—?"

"Just find a place away from the windows to sit and do your thing. I'll keep watch and make sure no one else comes by."

"You'll keep watch?" I asked, watching him move through the small room and take a seat by one of the windows. Red flags were waving high in the back of my mind, but my conscious brain kept pushing them away.

"Do you need anything before you start? Water, blood, food?" He had pulled a bottle of water and two bottles of blood out of a cargo pocket of his pants and was reaching into the pocket on the other leg before I had a chance to respond.

"The blood. Just the blood, please. Thanks." I hadn't even thought to bring anything to eat or drink.

"How much time do you think you'll need?"

"I don't know. I've never done this kind of thing before. I'm not sure how long it will take to—"

M grabbed my arm and yanked me into his body. I thought, for only a second, that he was going to kiss me. Then I saw the fire in his eyes. "A, it isn't safe," and he let go, grabbing the side of his head again, and moved across the room.

"What? What isn't safe?" He didn't answer. "M, what was that? What are you talking about?"

"Nothing. Sorry. I guess I'm just nervous." I could hear his heart pounding in his chest like a caged bird, but it didn't feel nervous, it felt eager— hungry. "Look, being here isn't safe. We need to hurry," he said.

"Yeah, OK." I pulled a cushion off the old dusty couch and tossed it into the corner to sit on. With the wall behind me I felt a little more secure—protected.

"Well, get on with it. We haven't got all night." When our eyes met, he started to stumble over his words. "I just mean, we both need to be back home before dawn. Otherwise, Iris might get suspicious."

"Right, suspicious." I hadn't told him that Iris already knew what I was doing, or that I had left her tied to a chair in her kitchen. If he found that out he just might think I'd gone mad.

I pulled my necklace out of my shirt and held onto the seer stone as I closed my eyes. I focused on C—Ciara—her ocean blue eyes and her fiery red hair, and I called out to her. Reaching out mentally, calling to her, and hoping she wouldn't fight me this time.

When I opened my eyes, I was there, in her small dirty room. But something was different. I felt different this time. I turned to find my reflection in the mirror across the room and came face-to-face with my own reflection—not Ciara's. "What the fuck?"

"A, what are you *doing* here!"

I turned around at the sound of her voice and saw C standing next to the window, as if she had been contemplating jumping and I had interrupted her. "You can see me?"

"Of course I can see you. You're standing right in front of me. What are you doing here?"

"I...I'm not sure."

"You can't be here. How did you even get past the guards?" Her eyes were wild, frantically shifting from me to the window and back again.

What was I supposed to say? I had no idea what had happened or how. Luckily, or maybe just by chance, I didn't have to answer, because Ciara suddenly lunged at me. I wasn't sure whether she meant me harm or just needed a hug. Either way, I reached out to accept her, but she went right through me as if I weren't really there. Tumbling to the floor, she hit the wall—hard. When she looked up, she was laughing. "You're not even real. I'm so delirious I'm having hallucinations."

"No, not a hallucination C. I'm here." *I'm here, I'm actually here.* It started to sink in, and I realized that this really wasn't like the other visions I had had. I wasn't physically there in the room with her. It wasn't teleportation like Councilman Ash could do, but I was there. Then it hit me: "Astral projection."

"What?"

"I can't explain it, I don't have time. But you have to trust me, OK?"

Standing, she came toward me, but she didn't say anything for the longest time. She reached out with her hand, trying to touch me but failing. "I—"

"C, look at me." She did. "Do you trust me?"

"Yeah." It was halfhearted but it was an answer.

"Then tell me you trust me. Please."

"I trust you." She didn't sound very convincing, but I didn't have time to try and reassure her. I needed to get her out of there and fast.

"Good. You need to come with me. The Council has declared a hunt to find you, and if I don't get you somewhere safe, soon, then they're going to open the hunt to all sector residents. That means—"

"That every lycanthrope and every vampire will be hunting me down in two night's time when the moon cycle starts." All the color, what little was left, just drained out of her cheeks. "I'm as good as dead."

"No, not if I can help it." I reached out to pull her up off the ground, but my hand went straight through her. "Shit!" I stomped my nonexistent foot on the floor and huffed. "C, I can't physically move you.

121

You have to help me. You have to do this on your own."

"I can't."

"Yes, you can. I'm here. I'll be with you the whole way."

Slowly, C started to stand, and I finally took in the extent of what had happened to her. Her arms had gotten frail and thin, her pant legs hung like loose skin, her cheeks were sunken in, and her hair—once vibrant, red, and full—was faded and limp, with a thick coat of dirt and grime. I wanted to scoop her up and protect her. I wanted to tell her that everything was going to be fine, that I would keep her safe. The problem was, I had no way of knowing what the actual outcome of all of this would be.

"Do you have any weapons?" I asked, hopefully. I knew none of mine would be of any help.

Good thing I brought along a small arsenal, I thought to myself.

"I have a knife."

"Good, keep it close, but don't use it unless I tell you to. OK?"

She nodded, pulling the knife out of her waistband and gripping it close to her chest.

"Come on, it's time." I pushed past her toward the door. It was shut, but that didn't matter. I stepped through. Looking left and then right, I saw that the hall was clear. I stepped back into the room and C was staring at me like she had just seen a ghost. "The hallway is empty. We need to go." She opened the door and together we made our way down the corridor and into a stairwell at the end.

I could hear voices, two or maybe three male voices, coming from one of the floors above us. *Or are they below us?* I wondered. *Are we walking into a trap?* I put my finger to my lips and C nodded in understanding.

14

Slowly, I led Ciara down the steps, one floor at a time. I hadn't realized we were so high up. When we finally reached the bottom floor—four levels down—I could see through the small dirty window in the door that there were, in fact, two men sitting in the entryway of the building.

I listened. Their heartbeats were slow and steady. Not as slow as a vampire's, but nowhere near as fast as a lycanthrope's either. "Humans," I whispered back to C. "They're just humans."

I stepped closer, planning to make my way through the door and out into the lobby, but C stopped me. "I can't."

"What?"

"I can't do it. A, I'm not like you. I—"

"What are you talking about? You love to fight, and they're just humans. You could take them with your eyes closed."

"No, not anymore. I've…I've seen things. I've changed. I'm too tired. I can't do this."

"Yes, you can. You have to. If they find you first, they'll kill you. They won't hesitate. They're human castaways. They're not even lycanthropes or vampires. To them, you're a monster. Besides, if you can't get past a few castaways, then there is no way you'll get back over the wall and into the sector."

"Into the sector?" Her eyes were wide with fear and filling quickly with tears. "A, I can't go back. I killed Wyatt. *I* did that. If I go back they'll kill me, you know they will."

"They won't kill you, I'll keep you safe."

"How?"

"I...I don't know, but I will. I promise."

She wasn't listening. I had lost her. She turned to look back up the stairs to the perceived safety of her four-walled cell. Without even thinking I reached out, as if to grab her shoulder, and pulled myself into her body. It was jarring—and an instant wave of nausea swept through me. I leaned over and threw up all over the bottom three stairs, dropping C's small knife to the floor in the process. I wiped off my mouth, C's mouth, with the back of her hand then stood back up.

"C, we have to do this."

I could feel her struggling to push me out, but I was in control now, and there was no way I was letting go.

I heard the hurried clatter of men's footsteps hammering their way toward me on the other side of the door. Apparently, they had heard me throwing up, or maybe it was the knife clanking around on the floor after I dropped it.

Bending down, I quickly picked up the knife, and threw my body against the wall behind the door just as it was swinging open. The two men tumbled in as if they were chasing someone, but when the first guy stopped abruptly the second one ran right into him, thrusting him forward and into the vomit I had just expelled.

"Sorry about that," I said with a smile, then I slipped out the door and ran for the exit before they even realized what had happened. I'd love to say that was the end of it, but no such luck.

Unfortunately, their little tumble in the stairwell didn't keep them down for long, and the two men were quickly out the door and chasing me down. Plus, their continuous yelling—"Get her!" "Vampire! She's a vampire!" and other such things—drew more attention than I had expected.

I ran down the street, realizing there were more buildings than had been indicated on the map.

Old map? Or was I just wrong about C's location? I wondered, but I didn't really have time to think about it. Thinking about it would lead to overanalyzing the fact that if I had been wrong then I now had no idea how to get back to the cabin. That would just freak me out, so I pushed the thoughts aside. Considering the fact that the two men were still chasing me, and other people had begun to slowly appear in the doorways and alcoves of the structures all around me, focusing on what was happening here and now around me was the better choice. Besides, I needed to move quickly.

It wasn't long before the humans had me surrounded. I counted ten in all: five men, two women, and three boys who couldn't have been older than eleven or twelve. I listened. All humans.

"I don't want to fight you." Ciara's voice came out scratchy, and her throat burned as I spoke. I realized that I/she was hungry. Where I had learned to control my hunger by drinking the bottled blood, Ciara hadn't had that luxury. I might not have wanted to fight them, but Ciara's instincts were much darker.

How long has she been out here, without blood?

"Too long." I could hear her answering the question in my mind and I knew it was true. This wasn't just a matter of being hungry; she was fighting to stay alive.

Suddenly I was afraid—petrified that her craving, her ravenous emptiness, might actually take over. I was trying to fight it, struggling to remain in control, but the sound of blood flowing through their veins echoed in my ears, and I could feel myself reaching out. I fought the urge that coursed through Ciara, to close the space between me and the man closest to me.

I didn't win that fight, Ciara did.

Ciara's body may have been small, frail even, but the human was still no match for her vampire speed and strength. I spun around him, and before he knew it I was at his back. I had my hands on the sides of his head. With a single movement, I twisted his neck, snapping it, and he crumpled, lifeless, to the ground.

The other four men came at me, while the women and young boys quickly backed away, moving toward the shelter of the closest building. I didn't have time to think, I just let my mind go so that my body— Ciara's body—could react.

"Fighting is 25% action and 75% reaction." Professor Gunner's instruction was finding its way to

the front of my mind--pushing through the hunger and helping me focus.

Growing up in Sector C, fighting was like second nature. You start taking hand-to-hand combat classes when you turn ten. No, I never fought five guys at once, but I was already *down* to four, so I decided that was a good sign. I reached out with my left hand and grabbed the shirt collar of the man who was approaching me from the left. When I turned, pulling him with me, I used his momentum to fling him past me and into the man coming at me on the other side. Their heads collided with a loud cracking sound, and I saw a thick splattering of blood as they both went down.

They wouldn't be getting up.

I was down to two, and neither one of them seemed all that confident anymore.

"Who's next?" I was breathing slowly, long deep breaths, trying to control my trembling hands. I was ready—ready for the next attacker.

At first I thought they would both attack together, realizing that I was getting tired, but neither of them stepped up. Instead, they both turned and ran into the closest building, slamming the door shut behind them. I could feel Ciara pushing at me, trying to force me out and this time I let her.

I was left, or at least my astral projected image was left, standing there watching as Ciara rushed over to one of the fallen men. I didn't even have a chance to object before she sank her teeth into the man's neck and began to drain him.

"Ciara, you can't do this," I begged. "You have to stop. We have to go."

She wouldn't listen. She was lost in her thirst and feeding her addiction. I scanned the buildings around us and could see eyes peering out through every window. We were far beyond outnumbered. I knew that if they got their courage back they wouldn't have a hard time winning against Ciara now. She was too far gone, and wouldn't even see them coming.

There was only one thing I could do. From behind her, I grabbed at her shoulder and pulled myself back into her. The taste of blood hit my tongue like an avalanche and for a second I didn't think I'd be able to fight it.

"NO!" I screamed as I pushed away from his dead body. "No, Ciara. Not now."

I stood up and forced myself to take back control. *"Look around Ciara,"* I begged, as I scanned the buildings again, forcing her to see what I saw. *"There are hundreds of them. They may not be coming for us now, but that doesn't mean they won't. We have to get out of here."* I could feel the realization of what was happening sink in. Her struggling stopped, and she gave over control to me.

Once I was sure Ciara wasn't going to fight me anymore, I considered my options. *"Do you know where we are?"* I asked her.

"No, I don't think so."

"You need to try, Ciara. Look around and tell me if there is anything you recognize from when you came here."

I slowly turned in circles, scanning the buildings to make sure no one was making a move, while studying the streets, the trees, everything.

"No…no, nothing." Ciera said it aloud.

"Talking to yourself, little lady?" I jumped at his voice, and turned to see a tall, muscular man stepping out from a darkened doorway and into the street.

"Nope, just heading…" *Where am I heading? Where am I heading?* "This way." I took off running, back in the direction we had come from. It was the only place Ciara knew, and the one place she felt remotely comfortable—safe. I could hear his heavy footsteps chasing me, but his size was more of a disadvantage at that moment, and I quickly outdistanced him.

Ciara and I slipped through the main doors of her building, and I gave her control again. Ciara's legs began to move, and I felt like a passenger, tagging along for the ride—like a kid being carried horseback. Had it not been a matter of life and death, I would have said this astral projection and body-sharing stuff was fun. However, seeing as I was pretty sure I had just killed three men and another was still chasing me, I wasn't going to go so far as to say I was having fun.

"Ciara, we can't actually stay here." She was moving toward the stairwell, and I knew she intended to lock herself up in that dirty little room of hers. *"He saw us come in. They'll be checking every room until they find us. Where else can we go? Where else have you been?"*

"Here, that's it." She stopped just short of the stairwell door. *"Wait. Next door. I can get us next door without all of them seeing."*

"Good. Go."

We ran down a long hallway that twisted and turned to the left then to the right, over and over again. The building hadn't looked that big from the outside, but then again I hadn't been paying too much attention. There was a doorway at the end of the hall, and Ciara quickly pulled it open and dashed down the stairs on the other side. I felt like I could tumble out of her at any moment, but I didn't.

When we made it to the bottom, she kept running, down a long dark tunnel. She was excited; I could feel it. The rush of energy I was feeling was all hers. I think I even felt a smile touch the sides of her lips. I wanted to encourage her, tell her I was proud, but I didn't. I was worried it might actually remind her of the danger we were in. It could have done more damage than good.

She stopped abruptly.

"What? What is it? Where are we?"

"Don't you hear it?" she asked.

"I..." I had been so caught up in the emotion of everything that I had stopped paying attention to what was going on around us—in the dark. *"Ciara, where are we?"*

"We're in the basement, an old tunnel connecting the buildings."

I blinked a couple of times, but couldn't really see anything more than shadows in the dark. Apparently, Ciara's night vision hadn't developed as much as mine had. Suddenly I missed my body. I missed the abilities I hadn't even appreciated fully. *"There's someone out there—in here, with us. Is that what you heard? Is that why you stopped?"*

"Yes."

I was hoping I had been wrong. No such luck.

"You're all alone. Frightened and scared in the dark. Wait, you're *not* alone, are you?" His voice echoed through the tunnel. I couldn't tell how far away he was. I wasn't sure if I had time to get away or if time was already working against me.

"How far Ciara?" How far to the door?" She reached back and I felt the doorknob under the skin of her fingertips. I grabbed ahold of it and turned quickly. As I pulled the door open, a burst of light came in from the other side, and I disappeared into it, pulling the door closed and locking it shut between him and me—us. I sucked in one deep breath after another, with my forehead resting on the door, until his body slammed into the opposite side causing me to jump back.

15

I could hear him screaming through the door. "This isn't over."

I knew he was right. It wouldn't be over until I got Ciara back into the sector, and maybe even then it wouldn't really be over. However, for now at least, he was on the other side of the door and I had Ciara safe and secure inside where there was at least light and—

"Well, well, well. What have we got here?"

"Shit." I slowly turned us around, pushing Ciara's back against the door, and was face-to-face with a room full of—I sniffed the air—"Vampires?"

"Very perceptive," said the tall, thin, blond-haired vampire who stood just in front of me. Not close enough to reach, but too close for comfort. There were at least two dozen others, vampires and lycanthropes together, scattered around the room. "You wouldn't happen to be the one stealing our blood supply now would you?"

"No. I swear, I never—" I stopped myself. I hadn't stolen anything, but that didn't mean Ciara hadn't.

"Ciara? Was it you?"

"I...yes, but only because I didn't know what else to do. I never meant to—"

"I get it. Just stop talking so I can figure this out." She was rambling. I had to stop her, but judging from the looks on the faces of the others around us I probably shouldn't have done it out loud.

"Are you talking to me?" the blond man asked, taking a step closer.

"No. Sorry, I...I wasn't talking to you, I was just..."

I was stuck between a rock and a hard place with nowhere to go. I had heard stories about the vampires and lycanthropes who lived in the wastelands, among the human castaways, as savages, but I never actually thought I'd ever have to face them. I hadn't prepared for this, not that I think you really could.

"I'm sorry. I didn't mean to bother you. I'm just... lost."

"Well, that's not really our problem, is it? You being in our territory, on the other hand, is." He took another step toward me and the crowd around him moved forward with him. He looked back over his shoulder, "What do you think everyone? Should we just let her go?"

The room shook with their laughter. Men and women alike, I could see it in their eyes, they wanted me dead. They wanted to be the ones to kill me.

"See," he said, turning back, "I don't think they want me to let you go."

He didn't wait for me to respond before he lunged forward, grabbing the collar of my shirt as I spun to the side. He yanked me back and threw me to the ground. I landed first on my backside and then smacked the side of my face on the cold, hard floor before rolling up and away toward the other side of the room.

"Hmmm, she's a feisty one. I'll give her that."

I almost made it to the door.

"Stop her," he yelled.

I would have made it if it hadn't been for the two rather large men who jumped in front of me just as I was reaching for the doorknob. "Where do you think you're going? We're just having a little fun," one of the men said, just before letting out the largest roar I had ever heard.

Lycanthrope, I realized as I sniffed the air around him. He smelt sweet, like candy. *Like Teagan and Micah*, I thought to myself. "Lion?"

"What's it to you?" he asked, and his eyes flashed a golden brown.

"Nothing. I'm just surprised you're, you know." I glanced over my shoulder at the blond man who was apparently their leader.

"A, don't do it," Ciara was warning me. *"Don't provoke him."*

"Do you always take orders from him? From a vampire," I said, needling him.

"I don't take orders from anyone."

"Oh, OK. My bad. It just seemed like maybe—"

He reached out and grabbed me by the throat. "I don't take orders!"

Before I even realized what was happening, I fell backward, pushed out of Ciara's body by the force of his hand around her throat. Ciara was stiff under his grip, but he dropped her as he and everyone else realized what had happened. "Where did you—? How did you get—?"

I probably could have explained it, but why bother.

"Ciara, get to the wall." I had to get her out of there, one way or another. I knew they couldn't hurt me. After all, I wasn't really there anyway, so staying behind wouldn't be an issue. *"Ciara, get to the wall."*

She stood there, like a statue, and whispered, "I can't."

"Get to the wall. I'll cause a distraction. You'll know what to do, I promise." She didn't move at first, but when she finally did no one tried to stop her. All eyes were on me.

She made it to the wall and turned back in time to watch as I stood up slowly, pushing back the nausea that was already starting to set in. When I looked up I met the blond man eye-to-eye. He gasped as he dropped to his knee and bowed his head, followed by all the other men and women in the room around him.

OK, that's not what I expected.

I had a flashback—a memory of a premonition. I was standing in the center of a crowd. There were vampires and lycanthropes all around me, intermingled. They were cheering. When I turned around, a woman with beautiful long red hair smiled at me. *'Don't give up. You have to fight this. You have to keep fighting,'* she said. *'I won't give up on you.'* The *woman* was squeezing my hand so hard it pulled me out of the premonition, and I was staring down at my hand, clutched in Ciara's as she squeezed it tightly.

"What is happening?" she asked.

I looked around at everyone, still on their knees. "I'm not sure."

16

That night, just as the sun had started to set, Ciara and I made our way quietly through the now-deserted town, but this time we weren't alone.

Isaac, the tall, thin, blond-haired vampire who was indeed the leader of the castaway gang we had encountered earlier that day was with us, along with Jabari, the werelion who had almost strangled Ciara with little effort at all, but this time they were on our side.

"Wait, stop. Over there," Ciara said, as she pointed off into the distance.

"What? What is it?"

"There's nothing over there but forest," Jabari said.

"No, that's not true. There's a trail, close to the wall. It's how I got out of the sector and found my way into the city," Ciara explained. "We need to go that way." She started running, and Isaac, Jabari, and I followed quickly behind.

We got to the edge of the tree line, and Ciara suddenly stopped. "It's here."

"What? Where?" I asked. If there was a trail, I couldn't see it.

"The path I took from the sector wall. There," she said, pointing off to her right. She was still—not quite the statuesque stillness that the old vampire can summon, but close. "A, if I do this, if I go back with you—"

"I'll keep you safe. I promise."

"We," Isaac corrected me.

"What?" Ciara asked.

"We will keep you safe," he clarified.

"You can't be serious. You can't go in there, they would kill you just for being castaways, let alone castaways who have entered the sector territory."

"But Micah instructed us: if we found you we were to protect you, no matter the cost," Jabari said.

"The cost would be your life, and if you lose that then you will be no good to me." I turned back to Ciara, who stood so still, gazing down the path that only she could see. "I will keep you safe. I promise," I reiterated.

"It isn't that, A. I just...don't blame yourself if you can't keep me safe. OK? Promise me you won't blame yourself."

"I will keep you safe, C. You and me, sisters forever."

"Sisters forever," she answered back.

Then, together, we took the next step and the one after that, with Isaac and Jabari following close behind. Soon we were at the edge of the sector, walking along the ten-foot concrete barricade that now separated us from our world inside and all the guards who were currently hunting for C.

Or did it?

17

"*A, you have to wake up. They're coming, and I need you to wake up. We have to get you out of here.*" M's voice was muffled—as if he were calling to me from the end of a long tunnel. I looked around but didn't see him anywhere.

"Did you hear that?"

"Hear what?" Ciara asked.

"Nothing, never mind." Just in my head then.

"*A, please. We have to get you out of here. We can't stay here any longer.*" He was begging. He was scared.

I couldn't help myself; I grabbed at C's shoulder. "I'm sorry C." Then, without warning I thrust myself into her back and started to run. I could hear Isaac and Jabari's heavy steps as they ran behind me, trying to keep up.

"*I'm coming. I'm coming.*" I ran as hard and as fast as I could. Up ahead I spotted a tree, close to the wall, with a low-hanging branch. In moments, I was scrambling up the tree and shimmying across the branch until I was just above the top of the wall.

"*A, this isn't a good idea,*" C pleaded.

"*A, wake up. You have to wake up,*" M was begging.

I knew C was right, but M was scared. I could hear it in his voice. I didn't have a choice, I had to go to him.

"I'm sorry C, but we have to do this. I will keep you safe, but I have to get to the cabin. Merick is in trouble." Scanning the woods on the other side of the wall, I couldn't see any guards, but I did see the cabin in the distance.

Thank the stars someone's on my side tonight.

I lowered myself down to the top of the wall, and turned back to Isaac and Jabari who were staring up at me like I was crazy. "Stay here. If I can get her back in safely I will; if not, we'll be back. Give me an hour, but if I'm not back by then, leave. I'll find a way to send word back."

"But—"

"No buts. This is how it has to be," I said, stopping him before he had a chance to finish his thought, much less his sentence.

Then I quickly jumped down off the wall and back into Sector C. The moment I landed, two things happened; I felt a burning sensation in my right wrist—Ciara's wrist, as her monitor turned back on, and I heard the sector sirens start up in the distance. I scanned the woods all around, but, from the ground, I could no longer see the cabin. Knowing the general direction I had to go I started running. *"I'm coming, M. I'm coming."* I tried to reach out to Merick, but with my body there in the cabin and my mind trapped in C's body I wasn't sure if he would be able to hear me. When he didn't answer, I knew.

I stopped short of the cabin by about thirty yards. It was quiet, undisturbed. Something didn't feel

141

right. Merick had been so frightened. I had heard it in his voice, but why? Why did he think they were coming? Were they already inside? I crouched down behind a large oak tree and listened—focusing on the cabin. Two heartbeats, mine and Merick's. We were still alone.

"Ciara, listen to me. I have to leave you now, but—"

"No, you can't. Please don't leave me." I could feel the panic building inside of her, and had to fight to keep it from taking over me too.

"Ciara, my body is there in that cabin. I've got to go to it, but you'll be all right. I promise. Stay here." I pulled some fallen branches over her legs and body, blocking her from any spying eyes. *"Give me fifteen minutes, and if I'm not back by then you come in through the back. Do you understand?"* She didn't answer, and I was afraid that if I left her she just might run back the way we had come. *"Ciara?"*

"I understand. Fifteen minutes. Through the back," she whispered. Her voice was trembling with apprehension, but I could feel her body beginning to relax.

"Right, fifteen minutes, and then you come in through the back. Don't forget." I don't remember closing my eyes, but when I opened them, I was curled up on a couch cushion in the corner of the dusty little cabin.

"Ghuahh." I came out of the vision with a gasp.

"Oh my stars, A, you're all right." M was inches from my face, pulling me up off the floor, but my legs didn't seem to work.

"I can't. Wait, give me a second." I needed time to breathe—to get my bearings. I was nauseous and dizzy, and my body didn't seem to fit right.

M didn't want to take *no* for an answer. He pulled me into his arms and started toward the door.

"We can't. C, we need to get C."

"It isn't safe. They know we're here. We'll have to try again later." He didn't understand. I realized he had no idea that I had already gotten to her.

"Outside. She's outside." The dizziness was starting to fade and I could feel my legs again. "Put me down. I need to go to her."

Just then the door opened and C stepped inside. Merick dropped me to my feet and put himself between me and Ciara before he realized who she was.

"Fifteen minutes, C. I said fifteen minutes. I needed time to explain—"

"Oh my stars, C? What happened to you?" Genuine concern flowed out of Merick as he reached out to her. Ciara crumpled to the floor and tears started streaming from her eyes. All the emotion of the past few days hit her like a punch in the stomach.

"Carry her." M didn't even question it. He scooped her up and was ready for whatever came next. "We need to get her back to your place."

OK, maybe he wasn't ready for that.

"My place? A, we can't take her to my place. She's a vampire. If she gets caught in the lycanthrope quarters, they'll—"

"It's the safest place for her. They won't think to look for her there. I'll stay over. If they smell a vampire, they'll just think it's me." His eyes were wide, and I saw the tiniest hint of a smile when I said I'd be staying too. "I'd rather deal with the Council thinking we're…you know, than have her get discovered. At least until I can come up with a better solution."

It was settled.

"Wait." I stopped Merick just as he was about to push the door open. "Did you say they know we're here?" All the color drained out of his face, and I knew it was true. "What happened?"

I could see it in his eyes: he didn't know. "It's like when I can hear your voice in my head, but it wasn't you, and it wasn't just a voice?"

"What do you mean?"

"It was like…like someone was literally controlling me, my body, how I moved—even the things I said."

"Like—" I started.

"Like you said you were able to do. I thought it was impossible, but I could feel it. It…it hurts."

"…We should probably do a perimeter check first." I had thought it was odd at the time, but brushed it off. "I'll go right. You go left. Stay at least twenty yards out at all times." Now Merick's odd behavior was starting to make sense: the way he had gotten angry when he found me near the cabin wall, before I had made it all the way around to the back side of the building.

It wasn't Merick.

It wasn't Merick.

"How long? How long were you not in control?"

"I don't know."

"Try to remember. When did you first feel it? When did you first realize something was wrong?"

"I—when we got to the cabin." He shook his head and rubbed his temple. "No, it was before that. After we got the weapons on and headed out, I think. I'm not sure. All I could do was watch as everything unfolded, like a nightmare. I felt…helpless." That one word said it all—helpless.

I was afraid to ask—afraid to know the answer, but I asked, "Do you know who it was?"

"No."

It had to have been a vampire, I had never heard of a lycanthrope having that kind of power, but *who*?

"When did it stop?"

"This morning," he said.

Morning? I thought. I glanced over his shoulders toward one of the dusty windows and sure enough the sun had started to rise off in the distance. *How long has it been,* I wondered.

"The sector sirens started going off, and I guess I was pulled out of it. They've been going off ever since. I've been trying to wake you, but you weren't budging. I thought…I thought I'd lost you."

"You didn't lose me. I'm right here. But this does change things. If they know you're helping me, then they probably know who we're protecting. That means we can't take Ciara back to your place."

"What?" Merick and Ciara asked simultaneously, as he set her down to step closer to me. Ciara's eyes had already started filling with tears.

"A, no. Whatever you're planning, you can't—"

"I'll have to take her back out. I'll stay with her there until after the moon cycle. Then we'll think of a way to get her back in," I explained.

"A, you can't stay out there, not during the hunt. Besides, you have no idea what's going to happen to you during the moon cycle," Merick pleaded.

"He's right," Ciara said. "If you end up turning, out there in the open, who knows what will happen. It's safer for you here, locked up with all the other new Lycanthropes." The logical Ciara I had grown up with and loved seemed to be finding her way back to the surface.

"I can handle it, I promise." In all reality, I had no idea if I could handle it or not, but they needed me to be strong, so I was. I turned back to Merick, "They'll never know I'm gone. Just go back to your place. If Iris comes looking for me tell her you haven't seen me, but that you'll send me home as soon as you do."

"But—"

"I got this, trust me." As I turned back to Ciara, a plan was already starting to form in my mind. "We need to *go,* and we need to hurry." I pushed open the door and started running. I didn't look back. I knew Ciara would be following, and that Merick would do exactly what I had asked him to do.

As we made our way back to the wall I tried not to think about what trouble Merick could get into on his way home. Lucky for us, the guards were focusing on the sector's main gates, and not the wooded areas throughout the sector. If they did, in fact, know we had been at the cabin, we had made it out long before they ever got there. When we were sure the coast was clear, I had Ciara lift me up to the top of the wall, and I pulled her up from there. Looking down, we saw that Isaac and Jabari were still standing there, waiting.

"You're still here," I said, actually surprised they had stuck around.

"Like I said, Micah told us to protect you," Jabari said.

I jumped down, and instantly felt a sharp, stinging pain run from my right wrist all the way up my arm. When I looked down, my monitor had turned off. "Oh crap."

18

"They had us all living in the community center. We each had our own room, and at first everything seemed great." Isaac, Jabari, and I sat quietly, listening while Ciara told us what she had been through since being released from Selection Week. "The first few nights we just stayed up late talking and sharing stories about Selection Week. We had a steady supply of bottled blood. The counselors gave us space. We were even allowed to use the gym and pool when the other residents weren't using it."

She got quiet, and took a long drink that emptied the blood bottle she had been grasping like a life raft. I handed her another one.

"What is it?" I asked.

"Nothing really. Things were fine. Everyone seemed to be doing well. They were controlling their hunger. I even thought I was."

"So what happened? How did you—?" I didn't want to say the words. I hadn't intended to ask how she had killed Wyatt or why, but I had to know.

"Uma was released first. She was told she could start classes at the medical center, as long as she kept a supply of blood with her at all times. Then it was Earnest. He was released to start his apprenticeship. I figured he wasn't going to be around too many people working as a records keeper…librarian…whatever."

"Wow, what a shit job," Jabari said.

"Not for him. Trust me, he'll love it," I said, remembering how happy E would get every time he got a new book to read. "E… Earnest…is a bookworm. Give him something to read and you wouldn't see him for days, until he'd finished it."

We sat there in silence for a few minutes, just thinking. Those were the good old days, back when our biggest worries were studying and taking tests. I would have given anything to be that young naive girl again.

Ciara opened the new bottle and took a long drink. "But then when Darius and Tamsin were both released and it was just me and Wyatt left, I didn't understand. I felt in control. I swear by the stars above, A. I really did feel in control." A single tear slid down her cheek and her lower lip started to tremble.

I slid over, on the couch, and wrapped my arms around her. "You don't have to do this. It's OK. You don't have to do this right now."

"Yes I do." She pulled away and sat up. "It was just Wyatt and me. While everyone else was off working, studying, doing whatever it was they were doing, Wyatt and I just hung out. We got close, you know." She laughed, a real laugh. "He's funny. I never realized how funny he is…was." She reached out and squeezed my hand. "Hey, I'm sorry. For all the crap I gave you back then. I was jealous of what you and M had. I just—"

"I get it." I knew what it felt like to discover someone. To *see* them for the first time. I thought back to that first day M had asked me to go get breakfast with him. I hadn't wanted to go, but C had made it impossible to say no. Looking back, I'm so thankful I did go. My life would have been so different if he hadn't been such a big part of it. We had found each other at a time that should have been all wrong, but it wasn't. Ciara and Wyatt had had that too, but for some reason it hadn't worked.

Ciara stood up, started pacing from one end of the room to the other and back again. "One night, Wyatt and I decided we were tired of being stuck in the community center. We just wanted to take a walk. I swear A, that's all we had planned on doing."

I reached out, gripping the arm of the couch and held my breath... anticipation? Maybe, but more likely fear. I knew what was coming. I needed to brace myself.

"There's a creek that runs through the sector. You know the one, it flows under the one-rope bridge." C was staring at me, waiting. I nodded. I knew the creek she was talking about. "We walked along the bank of the creek. I took my shoes off and walked along with my feet sinking into the wet earth, ankle deep in the cold water. The cold didn't bother me. I almost fell in a couple of times, but Wyatt caught me. He held my hand as he walked on the dry rocks alongside the water and helped me balance.

"We had been out there over an hour. I had almost forgotten why I had felt so cooped up in the first place. Then, I felt a sharp, stabbing pain, and the back of my leg went numb. I collapsed. Wyatt pulled me up into the grass. He was mumbling something about a snake, but I couldn't hear him clearly. His voice was muffled. When I looked down, there was blood covering my leg. I could see it, but I couldn't feel it. My head started to spin and then…everything went black."

"You passed out?" I asked, hopeful. *Maybe she didn't kill Wyatt after all. Maybe it wasn't her.*

"It must have been a water moccasin," Isaac said. "Their venom is actually poisonous to vampires. Lycanthropes can survive it for a while, but it will kill a vampire unless they're able to feed enough to wash the poison out."

"When I woke up, I was covered in blood. Wyatt was lying on the ground next to me, and he wasn't moving. I tried to wake him up, but when I rolled him over, I saw them—fang marks—in the middle of his left arm. I had drained him. His blood is probably what had saved my life."

"No probably about it. If you hadn't fed, you'd be dead," Isaac said. I'm sure he meant it as a comforting thought, but it wasn't.

"Yeah well, I might be alive, but he isn't. In the process of saving my own life, I took his." Tears were streaming down Ciara's face at that point, but she didn't make a sound. She sank to the floor. Her back to the wall, she just stared ahead. "I ran. I didn't know what else to do. I didn't have anyone to turn to. I just moved my legs one after the other and I kept running, all night. I made it over the wall and into that dirty little room without coming into contact with anyone. I never even heard anyone else in the halls for a few hours. I don't know what time it was when I got there. My monitor had turned off." When she looked down at her wrist, I realized I had been rubbing my own wrist too.

"It was like a lightning bolt had gone right through me, almost the instant I hit the ground on the other side of the wall." Her words described exactly what I had felt too. "But I didn't stop. I just kept running. I don't even know how long I was there before you came. Curled up on that mattress. I could hear noises outside and in the hallway. I locked the door behind me and just stayed there. I'm not sure how long. I left only once. When I went down to the basement. I found the tunnel. Then, I found the blood. I didn't mean to steal it, but I didn't know what else to do. No one was around and I was so thirsty. I took one bag, that's all. Then I ran straight back to the room and never left again. I was too...I just couldn't."

"You never left?" Isaac asked.

"No."

The realization of what she had gone through broke my heart. "You don't have to suffer like that any longer. I'll take care of you. I'll keep you safe."

She curled into a ball on the floor and, still crying, smiled. "You can't. You can't keep me safe. No one can." A few minutes later she was asleep, the weight of her secret finally off of her shoulders.

I sat there for what felt like forever before Isaac broke the silence. "I'm not sure that you'll be able to get her out of this one, but you are both welcome to stay here, with us for as long as you want."

He was right and I knew it. "Thank you, I appreciate it, but I still have to try," I said. "We'll stay through the moon cycle but, after that, I need to take her back."

"Then why don't you get some rest. I have a feeling you're going to need it."

I did as he instructed, and tried to make myself comfortable on the lumpy couch. It didn't take long for the sleep to come.

19

I awoke in the middle of the night to a sudden banging at the door. When I looked at my monitor, it said 1:37. *Wait, what?* I rolled over, forgetting that I had fallen asleep on a couch, and fell off, banging my knee on the table as I went down.

"Crap," I said out loud, but it wasn't my voice that came out, it was Merick's. *"Oh no."*

"What? Wait... A?" he asked.

"Yup," I answered. *How am I going to explain this?*

"What's going on, where are you? Why is my knee hurting?" M sat back down on the couch where he had been sleeping, and rubbed his knee, where I had banged it on the edge of the table.

"Sorry, that was me." Looking around the room I realized I had never seen his apartment before. *"Did you sleep on the couch?"*

"Yeah, I—"

Knock, knock, knock. Three more loud knocks at the door brought me—M—us—back to our feet. *"A, the door."*

"Yeah, I know. That's what woke me up," I explained.

"Um, about that. What were you doing in my mind while I was sleeping?"

Knock, knock, knock. I was thankful for the interruption this time. I didn't know how to answer his questions, and considering the dreams I had been having, I really didn't want to answer him.

I started toward the door, not sure who I was going to find on the other side.

"Where are you taking me?" he asked.

"We have to answer the door. Just act normal," I said as I reached for the doorknob. *"Actually, just let me do the talking."*

"It's cool, I got this," he said as he unlocked the door and pulled it open.

"Merick?" Iris asked as he/we pulled the door open just a crack to peek out.

"Yeah. Iris, what are you doing here?" he asked, in his usual casual, happy go lucky attitude. "What's up? Isn't it late?" He stretched his/our arms out and yawned before glancing down at his/our monitor. "No, wow, early. Why are you up so early? It's like the middle of the night."

Just stay calm. Just stay calm. Just stay calm. It was the mantra repeating itself over and over in my mind.

"Don't worry, I got this," he tried to reassure me.

"Please, please just let me do the talking."

"OK."

"OK? That's it?"

"Yeah, I didn't really care. I just like getting you excited."

"Oh... I'm going to kill—"

155

"Is Zelina here?" she asked as she pushed the door open and let herself in.

"What?" I asked, snapping back to reality.

"Where is she?"

"Hello to you too, Iris." I shut the door and crossed back to the couch. "She isn't here. Why would she be? Like I said, it's the middle of the night."

"If she isn't here, where is she?"

"I have no idea," I said. "I've been here, but if I see her I'll tell her you're—"

"Haven't you heard the sirens going off?" she asked.

I listened for a second, but couldn't hear anything so I crossed to the window, "What sirens?" I could play along too. "I haven't heard anything."

"Seriously A, those sirens have been going off all night, since before I left the cabin."

"I have a feeling they aren't going to stop any time soon," I said.

I pushed the window open, and the loud blaring from the sector-wide speaker system's *whoop, whoop, whoop* echoed throughout Merick's apartment. I quickly shut the window and turned back to Iris. "Oh, that siren. No, sorry, I hadn't heard it. Is everything OK?"

"Why were you sleeping on the couch?" she asked, as she lifted the bunched up blanket off the couch and held it out to me for a moment.

"I, um. It's just where I fell asleep, I guess," I said.

"Good question. Why are you sleeping on the couch?" I asked Merick.

156

"I don't know. It's just where I fell asleep, I guess."

"Smart ass!"

"Well, it's better than being a dumb ass," he answered, and I could feel the smirk spreading across his/our face.

"What are you smiling about? Are you even listening to me?" Iris interrupted our conversation.

"Yes, sorry. What were you saying?" I asked.

"Is she in your room?" she asked.

"What? No!"

Iris stormed across the room and burst through the bedroom door. I chased after her, but had to stop when I walked into the room. Everything was neat and tidy. The bed was perfectly made, books were arranged on the shelves from largest to smallest, and his clothes were neatly hung in the open closet along the far left wall. I had no idea Merick was so organized. The only thing out of place was an open chest under the window at the side of the bed.

"What's that for?" I asked him.

"My toys." I could feel the corners of his lips curling up at the thought of the weapons he kept hidden there.

Iris turned back to me, and I quickly wiped the smile from our face. "I told you. She isn't here. Now, can I go back to sleep or what?"

"Oh my stars, Merick. Focus, for just one minute please. It is not the middle of the night. It is 1:38 in the afternoon. You missed work today. I had to tell Haden and William that I asked you to do something for me just so they wouldn't start looking for you."

"You covered for me?"

"Yes. Well, I was covering for Zelina. I wasn't actually sure you were involved. Do you get it now? The guards will start gathering the new shifters to take them down to the holding cells at five o'clock, and I haven't seen Zelina since yesterday night when she left me in my kitchen tied to a chair with a gag in my mouth. So if you know where she is you need to tell me."

"You did what?" he asked.

"I, um. I'm sorry, but I really don't know," I said.

"Right. OK. Well, for the sake of figuring this out, let's pretend I believe you. Where do you think she would have gone to find Ciara?"

"Yeah, I don't know. Did you check your place?"

I could see the fire burning in the back of Iris's eyes, but the only way I was going to keep Merick out of this was to act dumb.

"Fine. Don't tell me." She turned and started toward the door. "There will be a guard waiting for you downstairs at five o'clock. They'll take you to the holding cells. I'll find Zelina on my own." She slammed the door behind her as she stormed out of the apartment.

"A, what are we going to do?" Merick asked.

"I don't know, but I'll think of something, I promise. Just promise me you will be downstairs at five o'clock. Don't keep them waiting or they'll figure out that you're involved in my disappearance. OK?"

He didn't answer me, and I could feel his mind working a mile a minute trying to come up with a solution.

"M, I'm safe, so don't worry about me. OK?"
"Yeah, OK."
"I have to go, but I'll see you soon."
"I Love—"

20

I didn't hear the rest of his sentence as I woke up, wondering if I had been dreaming or if I really had just been in Merick's mind. I looked down at my monitor, still off. I made my way across the dark room and flipped on the lights. Everyone was gone except Ciara, who was still sleeping curled up in a ball next to the wall, and me.

"You're awake," Isaac said from the doorway behind me.

"Yeah, sorry. What time is it?"

He lifted his wrists, "Sorry, no monitor here. Time doesn't really matter out here, you know."

"Right."

"Don't worry, I think we have an old clock that still works, down the hall."

He led me down the hall and into another smaller room where a few people were gathered, reading, playing old fashioned board games, and watching… "Is that, a television?" I had never actually seen one before; we aren't allowed to watch television in the sector, but I had heard stories.

"It is. Want to watch?"

"Yes. No, I mean I can't. I just need the time," I said, looking back at the screen where a group of teenagers were sitting in a dark cave drinking what looked like a goblet of blood. "What are they watching anyway?"

Isaac laughed. "Some old movie about vampires. I think that one's called 'The Lost Boys' or something like that. Either vampires used to be pretty weak, not able to go out in the sunlight or anything, or humans have seriously never understood us."

"Oh." The thought of not being able to go out into the sunlight seemed somehow sad.

"1:39."

"What?"

"The time, you asked what time it is. It's 1:39," he said again.

"In the afternoon?"

"Yes, in the afternoon. I thought about waking you guys up, but I figured you had been through enough and probably needed your sleep."

All I could think was that I needed to get back before five o'clock, when I was expected to be at the holding cells. Then it hit me—astral projection. "Oh my stars, that's a great idea."

"What's a great idea?" Jabari asked, as he and some woman I didn't recognize walked up behind me.

"I have no idea," Isaac answered. "I think she's talking to herself again."

"No, I'm just... Nothing, never mind. I need to go find Ciara. Thank you, and she'll explain later." I took off running, back toward the room where we had been sleeping. When I turned the corner into the room, Ciara was sitting on the couch stretching.

"Where did you go?" she asked.

"Nowhere, not yet anyway. I need to go back into the sector before—"

"But—"

"Don't worry, I won't leave you. At least I don't think so. If I do, it won't be for long."

"What are you babbling about? And what are you doing?"

I had started arranging pillows and blankets on the floor in the corner so I would have a place that was out of the way, to lie down. "Astral projection. It's how I found you yesterday. I think I can use it to make the guards believe I'm still there. That way, they don't come looking for me." I sat down and got comfortable.

"That's not going to work," Ciara said, as she lifted her wrist. "Still no monitor, remember."

I glanced down at my wrist. She was right. "Crap. I hadn't thought about that. If only I could teleport like Councilman Ash." I sat there defeated, but not for long. "I still have to try."

"Wait, Councilman Ash can teleport?" Ciara asked. "I didn't even think that was a real thing."

"Yeah, me either. I wouldn't believe it if I hadn't seen it with my own eyes, but it's true."

"Wow."

I just smiled. I liked seeing Ciara back to normal, or at least as close to it as I'd seen in the last few days.

I closed my eyes, took a few deep breaths, and focused on Merick, Iris, my bedroom back at Iris's apartment, and anything else I could think of. "How will I know if you're OK?" Ciara asked.

"I don't know, you'll just have to trust me. Try to keep it quiet in here, and just let me rest. I've only done this once before, so I'm not really sure what to tell you."

"Yeah, OK."

I could tell she was nervous, but I knew that Isaac and Jabari would keep her safe. Right now, I needed to focus on me and what I needed to do.

21

I opened my eyes and was standing in the middle of my bedroom back at Iris's apartment. I could hear voices coming from downstairs, but couldn't make out who was talking.

As I made my way down the hall, the voices became clearer. "She'll be here, I swear," Iris said. "She just went out for a run. I think she was feeling cooped up in the apartment all day."

Out for a run? She must be talking about me.

"Fine, we'll wait." It was Councilman Ash's voice.

We'll wait? Oh my stars what does Councilman Ash want with me, and who is he with?

"Wonderful." I could tell from Iris's voice that it was not in fact *wonderful.* "Would you like something to drink?" she asked.

"No," Ash replied.

"What about you Remy?"

Remy? As in Councilman Remy? As in the Sector C Leader? What is he doing here? I darted back into my room. *Just breathe, just breathe. You got this.* Looking at the mirror, I saw that I was in fact dressed for a run; at least she had given me a cover story.

How to get downstairs? I stood still, closed my eyes, and focused on the hallway outside of Iris's apartment. When I opened my eyes, there I was, just outside her door.

"Iris." I called to her, knowing I wasn't going to be able to open the door on my own. *"Iris, come to the door."* I knew it was a bad move to show all my cards in one move, but I had no other choice.

"Zelina?" she asked out loud—exactly what I had hoped she *wouldn't* do.

"Yes, Zelina, that is who we're waiting for," Ash replied.

"No, I mean—"

"Shhh. Don't say anything, just come to the door."

"I just mean, I thought I heard her. I'll be right back." I could hear Iris on the other side of the door, unlocking the deadbolt and turning the knob. "Where have you been?" she asked as soon as the door was open and she saw me standing there.

"Hi," I said, smiling. "I was out for a run. Why?"

Her eyes narrowed as she watched me squeeze past her and into the living room.

"Did you have a good run?" Remy asked, from his seat across the room. Ash was standing, motionless, about a foot behind him, as if on guard duty.

"I... We have visitors?"

"Yes, we have visitors," Iris repeated. The smile she wore didn't seem the least bit happy.

I edged into the room, stepping carefully between Iris and the chair where Remy sat, not wanting to get too close to either of them.

"I wasn't expecting so many people when I got home." I started toward the stairs. "Do you mind if I get cleaned up?"

I hadn't even blinked and Ash was gone. When I turned around he was there, between me and the stairs. "AAAAH!" I jumped back, tripping and falling right into the table in front of the couch. "Ouch! What the—? How did...?"

I'm corporeal. Oh my stars, I'm corporeal. Does that mean I can... Did I just use teleportation? Wait, if I'm here... I need to let Ciara know I'm OK. No! I scolded myself, *you need to focus on what's happening here, now. You can take care of Ciara later.*

"Stop scaring the girl," Remy said.

"It was not my intention to scare her," Ash answered. "I merely wanted to stop her from leaving. I thought it best that we talk now, rather than later, seeing as she'll need to go to the holding cells soon. He turned his gaze back on me, "Where did you run?"

"I... just along the back roads."

"Then why do I smell dirt, mud, and filth from the earth on you? Not to mention the blood," Ash added.

"I—"

Ash took another step closer. "Think carefully before you answer. You'll only get one chance."

"I... I'm not sure what you want me to say." I knew that Ash could get into my mind and find out exactly what he wanted to know, and that he probably had every intention of doing just that. But I wasn't going to make it easy for him.

Remy sat down and motioned to the seat across from him, "Please, have a seat. No one's going to hurt you here."

Yeah, right.

"I think I'd rather stand, thank you."

"I think you'd better sit," Iris whispered from inches behind me. "Please."

When I glanced back, she didn't look angry any more. Scared? Maybe. No, I think it was concern. *For me, or herself?* I wondered.

"Fine, but I'm not doing it because you want me to. I'm doing it because I'm tired."

"Very well," she conceded, and took a seat next to me on the couch. Ash stayed standing, of course.

22

Remy, in his naturally controlling, yet eerily calm manner, started. "You already know why we're here. So why don't you—"

"Actually I don't."

He closed his eyes and took a deep breath, one I knew he didn't really need. "The girl. We're here because of the girl. The one called Ciara."

"She isn't *called* Ciara. She *is* Ciara, that's her name."

"Zelina, please," Iris said as she grabbed my arm. "Mind your manners." I knew she was right, but I couldn't help myself.

"I—"

She didn't let me finish. She was probably worried what I would say. "I told you that there were others who felt the same way I do," Iris said.

When I looked up, Remy met my gaze. "You?"

"We," he corrected me, "and others."

"Others?" I looked from Remy to Iris; she just nodded.

When I looked back at Remy, he hadn't looked away, but he had gone still: that statuesque vampire still. He wasn't breathing—not that he needed to, but most of the vampires do it anyway. I think it makes them feel more human, not that they would admit that.

"I'm sorry." I didn't dare to look away from Remy again, or Ash. They seemed to fill the room with their presence, but I think my apology pleased Iris because she withdrew the death grip she had on my forearm.

"Iris, why don't you get us some drinks?" Remy asked, sitting back in his chair.

"But I…"

"The girl will be fine. No one will harm her; you know we need her."

They need me? To end the war? I wondered how he was going to try and sell me on the idea—if his pitch would be like Iris's pitch had been.

Iris did as she was asked and crossed into the kitchen, but I could hear her rushing to get the drinks from the refrigerator. In the process, there was a loud crash, and a mumble"— "shit"—followed by the rich smell of spilled blood and the sound of running water as Iris hurried to clean up the mess. A smile spread across Ash's face. He appeared to be taking delight in the discomfort and tension that filled the room. I was not.

"I'm sorry," Iris announced as she came back with three bottles of blood and one glass of water. She handed the bottles to Remy, Ash, and me, keeping the water for herself. She had wrapped a dish towel around her hand, and I noticed a distinctly sweet scent as she sat on the couch next to me.

Grrr. I heard a hushed, almost inaudible, growling noise. Looking around I wasn't sure where it had come from.

Did anyone else hear that? I wondered.

Ash was staring straight at me. He had heard it too, but he didn't say anything. Instead he looked down at the bottle in his hand like it was a foreign object, and sniffed at the top. "Ugh. It's putrid."

"It's not spoiled. I assure you it's still good," Iris said, trying to reassure him.

"Blood that comes from a bottle instead of a vein is always foul. It reeks of fetid flesh and lifeless prey." He set the bottle on the table and reached for Remy's. "Would you like me to find us something more suitable?"

"No, I'm all right. I'm not that hungry after all."

"It's the smell..." Ash continued as he set Remy's bottle on the table next to his. "It makes you lose your appetite. It will never compare to drinking it fresh."

I didn't agree, or maybe I was just too hungry to care. Maybe I just wanted to piss him off. I tipped the bottle back and quickly downed the contents. "Mmmm." I licked my lips then used the back of my hand to wipe off the blood that had escaped the sides of my mouth. "That does feel better. Thank you, Iris." I set my empty bottle on the table and leaned back against the couch cushions.

Grrr. The growling was louder this time, and when I looked up both Remy and Ash were staring at me. "What? It wasn't me."

Iris slowly rose from her seat next to me on the couch and backed away. "I think it *was* you, Zelina. It was your—"

"Her what?" Remy asked, standing now, but he wasn't moving away. He was coming closer, approaching me, as if he was eager to see—hear—more. "Can you tell if it was her wolf or her lion?"

"I'm not sure."

Iris backed further away, as if I were the threat. Ash just stared at me from where he had been standing, behind Remy's now-vacant seat.

"It wasn't me!" I demanded, but then it came again—louder this time and from the pit of my stomach. I clenched my hands around my throat and over my mouth, frightened it might happen again. All of a sudden I was afraid—terrified.

"She needs to eat," Iris barked.

"No, she needs to sleep," Ash corrected her as if bored with the conversation. "We don't have time to coddle an infant shifter."

"Sleep won't help her. It's not even two o'clock. It's too early for the change to come," Iris insisted. "Besides, if she sleeps you won't be able to question her about Ciara."

I turned to Remy, hoping for answers—hoping he would see a solution that neither Ash nor Iris had noticed. No such luck. He stood there silently, watching me, with an excited and almost pleased look in his eyes. "The guards will find the girl."

"But—"

"Iris." Remy cut her off. "This is more important. I wish to see what will happen."

Iris and Ash exchanged a long look. I don't think either one of them wanted to see what would happen, at least not sitting there in Iris's apartment. "Please let me feed her," Iris begged. "It's the only thing that can—"

"Have you forgotten—" Ash walked around to the front of the empty chair "—that the boy managed a partial shift while still in Selection Week? I'm afraid the usual rules don't apply to this one either."

"She needs to eat!" Iris was leaving the room and heading for the kitchen, "You don't know a thing about—"

Before she could finish, I saw a flash and Ash was gone. Then there was pressure on both sides of my head, and a sharp pain, as Ash thrust himself into my mind. Then he did what I could only describe as turning it off, and everyone disappeared.

23

I woke up on a cold concrete floor with a thin blue blanket and a flat pillow. It was cold. When I looked around, I realized I was in what could only be described as a cage.

Hmm, these must be the holding cells they've been talking about.

There were two concrete walls, one to my back and the other to my right, and two walls of tall floor to ceiling steel bars. The rest of the large square room was set up in rows of cage after cage—cell after cell. From where I was placed, in the back far corner, I counted four rows of four cages, sixteen in all, at least from what I could tell. It was hard to say where one cage ended and another began.

"Hello?"

Hello... Hello. My voice echoed back, and silence filled the room again.

"Hello? Iris, are you there?"

Iris, are you there?

I waited, but no one answered. The internal monitor on my wrist said 2:43. *At least I wasn't out that long,* I thought. Other than the kink in my neck, I didn't feel all that bad. "Ahem." I cleared my throat. It was dry, scratchy. Instantly I felt the burning

173

sensation that had recently become all too familiar—
hunger.

"Hello!"

"Are you hungry?"

It was Ash's voice, but he wasn't there. At least
not until I turned around, and then, there he was,
standing five feet behind me, between me and the
pillow and blanket I had left on the concrete floor. In
his hands was a tray with two bottles of blood and a
plate of what looked like raw meat."

"Is that...?"

"No." He vanished as quickly as he had
appeared. "It's mine."

I turned around again and he was standing on
the opposite side of the bars now, outside my cell,
tipping back one of the bottles as if he couldn't drink it
fast enough.

The burning grew worse, "Why are you doing
this?"

"'Why' is an excellent question."

"Is this some kind of game to you?"

"Not a game: a test. *Everything* is a test." Then
he was gone. I had turned before he had a chance to
reappear and rushed to the spot he had vacated only
moments before. As soon as he materialized I
grabbed the remaining bottle off of the tray and
started drinking. It was warm on my tongue, not cold
like the bottled blood that Britt and Iris gave me.
"Exquisite," he said as he smiled—no, smirked. I
could tell by his reaction that he was in fact impressed
that I had gotten the bottle off the tray before he could
stop me.

The blood was gone in seconds, but I was still hungry. I reached for the meat but stopped short. "Is it... raw?" The thought made my stomach churn, and I was sure I was going to gag.

"It is," he answered as he watched me carefully and all too closely. "Go on, try it."

I reached for it again, but just as the tips of my fingers touched the still warm, wet meat I felt nauseated. "I...I can't."

Grrr.

"Your beast disagrees." He smiled.

Grrr. He was right. The beasts—wolf and lion— growled from somewhere deep inside of me. They wanted the meat, and it didn't matter how much it repulsed me. Without even thinking I reached out, grabbed the raw steak, and took a big bite. Blood dripped down the side of my mouth, and in seconds the steak was gone. I looked up, but Ash was gone too. I didn't see anyone else around, so I licked my fingers clean.

"Zelina?" I turned and saw Iris walking in, followed by Ash and Remy. "Are you all right?" their footsteps echoed in the room as they made their way to the back corner where I stood with my back to the wall.

"I'm all right," and I realized I actually was. *Maybe Ash had been right, maybe all I had needed was a little sleep.*

They stood outside of my cell—my cage. Ash didn't teleport this time. No games—no *tests?* I wondered.

I watched Iris through the bars, but she didn't speak. I broke the silence. "What is this place?"

"It's where we bring the new lycanthropes. It's a safe place for them to shift during their first few moon cycles."

"Safe maybe, but definitely not comfortable." I looked back over my shoulder at the thin blanket and the limp pillow.

"Comfort isn't really the first thing on your mind when you're learning to shift. Hardly anyone is able to sleep, nor do they want to."

I thought about that. Over the years, I hadn't actually given much thought to what lycanthropes go through during their transformation. The only lycanthrope I had ever actually seen transform was Micah, and that was a forced change when the guards had shocked him with their tasers during our Selection Week fight. His shifting had been fast, wet, and awful. The thought of going through that—I couldn't imagine.

"What does happen?"

"I..."

"Prepare the girl," Remy said, pushing Iris to continue.

"What do you want to know?" Iris asked.

"I don't know. Will it hurt? How long will it last? How does it happen? Anything. Just tell me anything. Please."

"It's painful, the first few times." She reached out and held onto the bars of my cage, remembering. "Actually, it's always painful. That doesn't change, but you do get used to it. Your muscles and your bones feel like they're stretching—moving. It's unnatural. Your entire body moves at once, pulling the skin to move with it and allowing the beast to take control.

You can't control it, not at first, but in time you will. Eventually, you'll be able to shift whenever you want. The moon cycle won't have any control over you or your beast. The more you shift, the quicker you'll be able to do it. That alone will help you deal with the pain."

"Then why...?" *What do I want to know, what do I want to know?* "Why do the lycanthropes only hunt during the moon cycle?"

"Sector law." She glanced back at Remy, our Sector Leader, and I wondered what she was thinking. For a moment, I thought about jumping into her mind, but then thought better of it. "We can shift whenever we want, but we can only feed—*hunt*—during the three days of the moon cycle." Her eyes changed, just for a moment, to a brilliant yellow, almost amber, and I could picture her tiger coming to life around them.

"The girl will be fine. No one will harm her. You know we need her." Remy's words from earlier came back to me.

I turned to Remy, who, as always, seemed to ooze confidence and power. I'm not sure if it was his clothing or the way he held himself, but instantly I felt little—insignificant. "Can I ask you something?"

"Of course."

"You're the Sector Leader; why would you want to dissolve the Governing Council?" I asked him directly, without breaking eye contact. I didn't want him to see how nervous I actually was.

He didn't seem to be surprised by my question. None of them did. "The time has come for change. I believe—*we* believe—that in you, in your ability to withstand both the vampire virus and the lycanthropy virus, we have found the answer to the divided races."

"What does that even mean?"

"It means that…we believe that, given time, we could find a way to combine the viruses, to create one race. A superior, hybrid race. One society that can survive without destroying itself. We wouldn't feed off of each other because we would all be the same. We wouldn't be in a constant struggle for leadership—for power. We would be derived out of the best parts of everyone."

"Hasn't society tried that and failed before?" I asked. He watched me closely, but didn't answer. I took a breath and continued. "Wars have been started because one group of people believed they were the superior race. People have been killed just because they were different. Even vampires and lycanthropes were once persecuted, hunted, and killed, because society thought we were abominations. What makes you think that now, after so many have failed before, you have the secret to the perfect race?"

"You will fail at everything you do not try," he said quietly.

"And if all of that were even possible, what would you need from me?" I asked.

"Well…" Iris began, "if you are the one, if you are in fact a hybrid, then we'll need to run some more tests. According to our records there has never been a real hybrid, at least not within the sectors. There is so much we don't know. There is so much we need to understand about what that actually means. We'll need to find out what's different about the way the viruses react to your blood, why they both are able to survive in your system. Then, eventually, we'll need to find a way to combine your blood with the blood of other vampires and lycanthropes."

"You'll need my cooperation."

They exchanged looks, but Remy was the one to speak. "We'd like it, yes."

"And what do I get out of it?"

"What would you like?"

Freedom, I thought to myself, but I knew that wasn't going to happen. "I want..." *What do I want?*

"I'm listening," Remy said, and he was.

"Ciara," I said without really thinking it through, but I met Remy's gaze straight on and didn't back down. "I want you to leave her alone, or I won't help you."

"I can't—"

I didn't let him finish. I didn't care what he had to say. If I was going to go down this road, then I had to commit, fully. "If you want my help, you'll leave her alone. You'll cancel the hunt and make sure she is kept safe. Here. In the sector." Looking around, I had a moment of clarity. "And not in a cage. She goes free."

"What makes you think we haven't found her already?" Ash asked as he stepped forward.

He's right, for all I knew they could have already found her, convicted her, and killed her. "If you had found her, you wouldn't be here with me, wondering if I know where she is," I bluffed.

"Who says we—?"

I didn't bother so much as a second glance in Ash's direction. Remy was the one I needed to convince. "You don't have her. I know you don't. So,

I'm telling you, if you want my help you will stop looking. You will keep her name out of all the records, and no one will know she was even a suspect in Wyatt's death. And if the guard members already know that she is the one they've been hunting, then you will make sure each and every one of them knows she is no longer to be punished."

"If I do that, my leadership will be questioned. You can't possibly expect—"

"What I expect, is that you will do, for your people, whatever is necessary to achieve your goal."

"Fine, but I can't cancel the hunt." I started to argue, but he cut me off. "What I can do, is order her found and brought before the Council."

"So they can punish her? That's not what—"

"So that I can be the one to determine her fate. As long as the sector residents see that she has been taken into custody and that the Council is determining her fate, I can control the outcome. The residents will be satisfied, and upon her release no one will question my orders."

"Not while I'm in here. You have to wait till I'm out so I can stand by her side."

"I will not wait. It will happen as soon as the girl is found." He paused. I wondered what he was thinking, but I didn't think it was safe to peek into his mind. "I will assure you, when the time comes, no harm will come to her."

I didn't entirely trust him. I wanted reassurance, a promise, a guarantee, but I knew this was probably as good as I was going to get.

If you are the one… If you are the one… Iris's words found their way to the front of my thoughts.

"And if I'm not *the one*?" I asked, turning my attention back to Iris, who stared back at me in shock.

"I'm sorry?"

"You said, 'if you are the one.' What happens if I'm not the one?"

"Then we keep looking."

It was as simple as that. It was either me or it wasn't, but, if it wasn't me they weren't going to stop looking until they found *the one*.

"How will you know if it's me?"

"You'll change. Either your wolf or your lion will take possession and you'll transform. Tonight."

I wanted to tell her I wasn't ready, that they had the wrong person, and that there was no way I was going to change, but even I knew that wasn't true. I could already feel the beasts living inside of me. I could feel them struggling to get out. "Wait!" It hit me like a ton of bricks. I could feel them struggling to get out. Fighting each other. *Why had I not realized it before?* "How can I... What if both of my... What will happen to me?"

They all knew what I was asking, but none of them had the answer.

"You will be torn apart. Literally," Ash said without blinking. Part of me wondered if he was secretly hoping I would be torn apart.

"But we don't believe that's going to happen, Zelina," Iris hastened to add. "The odds of that are so slim that it isn't even worth discussing. Before Britt was—" She stopped herself. "Before she left, Brit made detailed notes on your charts. She said that your blood work was showing aggressive strains of both the vampirism virus and the wolf virus. Although she did see hints of the lion virus, she noted that it was insignificant in comparison. So you see, there is nothing to worry about."

I wanted to believe her, I did, but I knew better. I could feel the wolf and the lion inside of me, equally powerful, worming their way closer and closer to the surface. It was only a matter of time before one or both of them made their way through.

Iris must have understood my doubtful expression. "I need to talk to Zelina, alone, please," she said. No one moved. "Please." Remy and Ash nodded, and made their way out of the room.

24

I knew that both Remy and Ash could probably still hear us talking, from out in the hallway, but I didn't care. With them out of the room at least we had the illusion of privacy.

"I know it's a lot to take in all at once, but…"

"I don't trust him," I said.

"Who?"

"Remy. I know you say he's on your side—my side—our side—but he was willing to banish me after Selection Week—"

"But he didn't."

"I know he didn't, but he thought about it." She opened her mouth like she was going to argue again, but I didn't let her. "I can't explain it. I just don't trust him, not entirely."

"I've known him for a long time. This is something we've—he's—wanted for a long time."

I was pacing back and forth in my cage. My muscles were aching, and the movement seemed to help. "How can you be so sure?"

"You weren't there, Zelina. You didn't see how he reacted when he found out about you."

"Then tell me." I stopped right in front of her, gripping the bars in my hands and looked deep into her eyes hoping to see the truth. "Make me believe, as you do, because I want to believe. I really do."

"It's better if I just show you."

"Show me?" *What is she talking about?* "How can you show me?"

She looked down, fiddling with her hands. "I know what you can do. I know you have visions, even premonitions. I had no idea the extent of what you could do until earlier today, at the apartment, but I do know."

"I don't know what—"

"It's OK, you're not in trouble. I'm not going to tell anyone…" Our eyes met again. "Anyone who doesn't already know."

"Who knows? Other than you, I mean."

"Teagan knows, but you already knew that. Britt knew, but she's gone. She doesn't matter anymore." There was a sadness in her eyes that I wasn't used to seeing.

"You miss her, don't you?"

"She was a friend—an acquaintance. Nothing more."

I didn't think that Britt liked any of the shifters, but I let it go. "Who else?"

"Both Remy and Ash know, and a few others. All friends—supporters."

I couldn't believe what I was hearing. Remy, the leader of Sector C, knew that I get visions and premonitions. People have been banished, even killed, for having visions and yet here I was, being kept safe—even if it was in a cage—for my first moon cycle. The most powerful and influential person in the sector knew what I could do. I'm not sure how I felt about that.

"Right, supporters."

"I know you don't believe me, but you will." She reached between the bars. "Here, take my hands." I did. "Close your eyes. I was at home when I got the call."

What call? I wondered, until I heard the ringing. Ring-Ring-Ring.

I opened my eyes and I was there, sitting at the kitchen table in Iris's apartment. There was a plate of eggs, steak, and bread in front of me, and I could feel how hungry I was—she was. It was still dark outside, so I could clearly see my reflection in the window above the sink—Iris's reflection, not mine.

Ring-Ring-Ring.

I stood and crossed to the phone. Picking it up I wasn't sure what I was supposed to say, but it didn't matter because Remy's voice broke the silence, "My office. Now."

I looked down and saw that I was still in my pajamas.

Hmmm. Iris wears pink pajamas? I thought to myself. I didn't even know we could get pink pajamas in Sector C.

I headed up the stairs to Iris's room to change, but when I opened her bedroom door, I stepped into Remy's office instead.

What the…?

I quickly looked down, and was relieved when I saw that the pink pajamas I had been wearing were now replaced with a pair of blue pants and a light blue shirt I had seen Iris wear a hundred times before.

"Good, you're here," Remy said, as I stood there. "Come in."

I did as I was told and shut the door behind me. Sitting in the chair across from his I tried to act as normal as possible, but my heart was racing in my chest. I had no idea what to expect. "What's going on? What was so urgent?"

"It's happened. It's finally happened."

"What's happened?" I asked.

"Teagan called me early this morning. The girl survived."

"The girl..."

"C65A53, the one who fought yesterday. She was scratched by the young wolf. We're still not sure how he was able to do a partial transformation but no matter—she survived—and to top it off, she has both vampire and lycanthrope viruses active in her bloodstream."

I just sat there. He was talking about me. I knew it, he had said my name, but somehow it just seemed so unreal.

"It's what we've always hoped for," Remy said as he grabbed my shoulders. "Now, maybe we can start making the changes we need for us to be together. Really together. No more hiding. No more of you running around with that..." His face contorted unnaturally. "That wolf."

I pulled away without even thinking about it. "He has a name," I scolded, before I could stop myself. "Besides, we aren't running around. We're friends, and you trust him. I know you do." Somehow, I don't know how, but I knew I was right.

"He isn't on our side, not yet. That was your job. Once that's done, I'll trust him. Until then, he's just another obstacle."

"Haden is my friend. Whether you like him or not doesn't matter. My friendship with him doesn't affect how I feel about our plans either."

"*Our* plans?"

"Yes, our plans. We will see this thing through to the end. We will unite the vampires and the lycanthropes, just like we've always wanted. After that..." I/Iris stood, pulling away from Remy's grip. "After that, I don't know. We'll just have to see. Keep me posted." I/she turned away, and everything went black.

When I opened my eyes, I was standing face-to-face with Iris, with only the bars of my cage between us. "Now do you believe me? He wants this just as much as I do."

"Maybe a little more."

"What do you mean?" She let go of the bars and casually backed away.

"I mean, he has something he's fighting for, but you don't. Maybe you did when you started this, but you don't have the same feelings you once did. I can feel it. You don't love him, not the same way he loves you."

"He doesn't lov—"

"Yes, he does. You're kidding yourself if you think he doesn't."

"Do you believe me now?"

"I believe you."

"Good."

"What happens when he finds out?" She didn't look back. "Are you even planning to tell him?"

"That's none of your concern, Zelina." She started to leave, but stopped. "I need to ask you something."

"What?" I asked.

"Back at the apartment, what was that? The way I heard you…not through the door, but in my head."

"I'm not sure."

"Are you lying?"

"I…it's complicated," I said, not knowing what else to say.

"I'm sure it is. I suppose now isn't the time to talk about it, but soon enough you're going to have to trust me enough to talk."

"I will—I mean, I do." *No, I really don't.*

She left, and I was alone, again.

25

The other lycanthropes from my selection class were brought into the holding cells a few hours later.

"Oh my stars, A, what are you doing here?" J, or Jade as she is now called, was brought in first, just before lunch time, led by a short, stocky guy who looked like he would rather be anywhere but there.

"Same as you, I guess."

"Wow, crazy right?"

"Yeah, crazy." I watched as he put her in a cage along the back wall, across from me but two rows over.

The guard handed her a thin blue blanket and flat pillow just like the ones I had woken up with. "These are yours. Try not to destroy them." Then he was gone, down the row and out the door with no more instruction than that.

"Jade, you do know what's happening, right?"

Her brown eyes lit up and a smile spread from ear to ear, across her face. It was the same look she always got just before stepping onto the fighting mat. She was an adventurer, one of the boys. That's why she fit in so well as the first female ever to be assigned to the External Security team. I should have known she would see this as just another adventure.

"Of course, we all do," Jade said. "Right after Selection Week the elders brought all of us here. They told us we'd be staying here during our first few moon cycles. They explained why, and told us what to expect. It seemed pretty straightforward, and other than the uncomfortable digs it doesn't seem all that bad. It's like camping."

"Not all that bad? Camping? Are you sure they told you everything?"

"Yeah, why?"

Before I had a chance to answer, F, Forrest, was led in, and I had lost Jade's attention completely. The guard put him in the cage next to Jade, the third one in the second row. "These are yours. Try not to destroy them." He tossed the blanket and pillow into the cage and left.

Forrest and Jade just stood there, holding hands through the bars like star-crossed lovers. "Did you two…?"

"What?"

"Nothing, never mind." I wanted to ask if they had filed a family unit application, but decided against it. I had never noticed, until that moment, how much they looked alike. His wavy, dark brown hair was shorter than hers, reaching only to his shoulders, but it was just as shiny and I imagined just as soft. I wondered if something in their appearance had changed since becoming weretigers, or if the similarities had always been there.

Nash was brought in next. I won't lie, I was glad when the guard locked him up in the first cage into the room and closest to the door. He was three rows away from me and on the opposite end of the room. Every time I thought of him I remembered the way he had spied on Merick and me and all the things he must have told the Council. Images of the picture I had found in my room flashed through my mind. Don't get me wrong, I love the photograph, but the idea that he might have taken it to give to the Council really pisses me off. Maybe it wasn't completely his fault. Councilman Serenity should take some of the blame, seeing as she was the one who told him to follow me. Even so, I couldn't help but blame him for everything that had happened, and was happening, to me. I half hoped he wouldn't get a blanket and pillow, but no such luck.

"These are yours. Try not to destroy them."

I was beginning to think those were the only words the guard knew.

Quinn and Riker came in next. They were talking and laughing with the guard.

What? Wait a minute, he does have a personality?

It was the first time he had smiled since he started escorting people in.

Riker held his arms out and leaped into his cage as if he had already turned. "Riker's in the house, let the party begin!"

"Huh. You know the party can't start without me," Quinn corrected him.

Typical, I thought to myself, as I watched the two of them strut around in their cages. Both Quinn and Riker seemed to have gained another fifteen to twenty pounds since the last time I had seen them, and it was all muscle. They were really beginning to look like bears, at least in terms of size. Neither one was particularly hairy in any way, though. I was afraid to know what they would look like after they transformed. Naked bears—it wasn't a sight I was particularly looking forward to. Quinn was put in the cage directly behind Forrest. Riker was kitty-corner to Forrest and sandwiched between Quinn and Nash.

"Hey A," Riker called from his cage. "What are you doing here? Don't they have a special place for all you fangers?"

"I don't know. I guess they just thought they needed someone here to keep you in line tonight."

He laughed, from the gut. "You think you can keep me in line? That's rich."

I didn't bother responding. Not when a simple smile said it all and got under his skin in the process.

"There must be some reason they're keeping her all the way in the back corner," Jade said with a laugh.

"Yeah, so when I break the bars of my cage she'll be trapped."

Jade just shook her head. "That's the only advantage you'd get in a fight with A."

"What? Are you a fang lover now Jade?"

"No, but A's not just a fanger." She looked over and smiled at me. "We girls gotta stick together, right?"

"Right." I couldn't help but smile back. Jade and I have never been real close. It's not that I didn't like her, I did. It's just that she always preferred hanging out with the guys. Who was I to judge?

"Forget about her," Quinn said. "After tonight, when she fails to change, everything will go back to the way it's supposed to be. People will stop talking about her, and they'll stop freaking out about changes in this and changes in that, Council secrets, and Council cover-ups as if the end of times is coming."

The end of times?

"It's ridiculous what people are saying," Quinn continued. "I don't believe in omens or signs or any of that crap. She is just a vampire. The sector is full of them, too many if you ask me."

"Yeah, you're right," Riker said, taking a seat on his cold concrete bench. "Fucking fangers."

Merick and Hudson were the only two lycanthropes left. So, when they brought Merick in and put him in the cell next to mine, I couldn't have been happier. We were the only ones in the fourth row, with everyone else in the first two. It didn't go unnoticed.

"Hey."

"Hey yourself." He grabbed the bars between us at the same time as me. "How are you here?" he whispered, not wanting anyone else to overhear.

"Honestly, I don't really know."

"What does that even mean?"

"OK, this is going to sound crazy, I know, but did we... Was I...?"

He leaned in closer. "So that really did happen?"

"Oh my stars, it wasn't a dream then." I let out a breath I hadn't even known I was holding. "I wasn't sure if it was a premonition, or a vision, or.... It's never felt like..."

"What happened with Iris?" he asked. "You know, after all that stuff, after you left."

"I... I made it back to her place, just in time to see Remy and Ash before they sent the dogs after me. I almost got caught. Not *caught-caught*, but they almost found out I was...using astral pro—"

"Projection? Astral projection? A, how?" His voice raised, attracting the attention of the others, who stopped talking to watch us.

"Wow," Jade said, pulling away from Forrest, and staring across the aisle at me. "What is with the steamy tension over there?"

"What are you talking about?" I asked.

"You two. When did you become a thing?"

"I—we—"

Saved by the bell, so to speak. William and Haden, my own personal bodyguards, walked in following H, Hudson. They locked Hudson into his cage, the one across from Nash, and tossed him his blanket and pillow. "Here," William grunted. "The guard said these are yours, try not to tear them up or something."

Then, they each placed a seat outside of my cage and got comfortable.

William took out a deck of cards and began shuffling. "Game?"

"Sure." They started playing as if this was the most normal thing in the world.

"Are you going to stay there all night?" I asked.

"Yup," Haden answered, not even bothering to look up.

"I'm behind bars. What could I possibly do in here?" I asked.

"Don't know. Don't care," Haden answered.

"Great, just great," I mumbled under my breath. I knew I was going to need a distraction. I turned my attention back to M. *"I need to get back to Ciara, M. She has no idea what's happened to me. Can you cause a distraction… help me take William and Haden's minds off me?"*

As if on cue, Riker opened his mouth to cause his own little scene, and I, unfortunately, was at the center of it. "Ha-ha. What's with the babysitters, A? Afraid to be alone with us?"

"Actually Riker, I think they're afraid to leave *you* alone with *me*. If I had to guess, it isn't my safety they're worried about."

William chuckled, then coughed, trying to cover it up.

"There are a lot of young shifters in this room, Zelina." Haden cautioned me. "Don't forget they won't be behind bars forever."

Was that a warning? I wondered.

"Enough," William said. "It's going to be a long night as it is. The last thing we need is for them to start fighting. I don't want to deal with that; it's not what I signed up for."

"You didn't sign up," Haden reminded him. "You were assigned. That means whatever happens, instigated or not, gets dealt with."

I wasn't sure I wanted to know what he meant by "gets dealt with," but I didn't really have time to think about it. Things started happening pretty fast after that.

I remember hearing Hudson first, crying out in pain, and then it was Jade, Nash, and Forrest.

"Hmmm, I would have guessed she'd have cracked first," Haden whispered to William as he nodded in my direction.

"I can hear you, you know."

Quinn and Riker held out as long as they could, grunting and taking deep breaths through the pain, but it didn't last—not long. Eventually, the whole room was filled with screams of agony—pain—even terror.

Even Merrick had doubled over and was gripping his sides as he squirmed across the floor of his cage.

I reached out to him, through the bars of the cage. "Merick? Can you hear me? Everything's going to be all right."

He didn't answer. He didn't even look at me. He was lost in the agony.

"Merick? Are you all right?"

"I'm... it hurts. I knew it would hurt, but this—this is bad, A." It wasn't the answer I was hoping for, but at least he was able to answer.

"What's happening? What's wrong with them?"

"Nothing's wrong," Haden said, laying his cards down. "Didn't they explain to you what would happen?"

"Yes... No... I guess, but I didn't think..." *I didn't realize it would be like this.*

Then it happened.

26

It started in my throat, an intense burning hunger. It was different from the hunger I get when I need blood, this was primal—animalistic. Then it became physical, starting with my skin. The itching and stinging. It felt like my skin was too tight for my body. Dry and on fire, the pain got worse. I bit my lips to keep from crying out. I tried to focus, to take my mind off the pain. Looking around the room, I noticed that none of the others seemed to be experiencing the same thing as me. They were all still crawling across their cage floors, moaning in pain.

Does that mean my pain will only get worse? I wondered.

Most of the others had only partially transformed. Half-dressed and half undressed I could see fur starting to spread across their arms, legs and backs. All except Quinn. Quinn was stretching tall in his cage. He was almost entirely transformed, and I could see that he was able to reach nearly to the top of the bars. He wasn't screaming anymore. There was a peaceful, almost tranquil look on his face. I wondered what he was thinking, but only briefly, because the pain came back.

Oh my stars, I thought for only a second before another wave of pain seared my skin. The burning deepened, and I tore at my clothes, throwing them to the floor.

"Show's starting," Haden announced.

I could hear William grumble and pictured him shaking his head, but I didn't turn to look. "You're sick, you know that, right?"

I watched as the light blond hairs spread across my arms and legs and grew thicker, darker, until they were a chocolate brown.

The muscles in my arms and legs started to throb. If you can imagine a leg cramp, it was like that only a thousand times worse. My entire body was cramping. All the muscles seizing and contracting at once. I reached out and grasped the metal bars of my cage, trying desperately not to fall, but it was no use. I dropped to my knees and screamed out as the muscles, first in my hands and feet and then in my arms and legs, began to contort.

"What do you want to bet she doesn't complete her transformation?" I heard Haden laugh.

"She'll complete it," William said, and I could feel his eyes on me without even looking.

"Then at least bet me on what she'll be, wolf or lion."

"Ahhhh!" The pain was too much. "Shut the fuck up," I snarled.

Suddenly my vision blurred, and the room went quiet, except that it didn't. When I was able to focus again, I could see through the bars that Merick was still shifting—still screaming out—but I couldn't hear him.

I can't hear. I can't hear? The idea should have terrified me, but it didn't. If it wasn't for the pain I was in, I think I would have actually laughed.

I could feel my muscles growing, stretching, and expanding. I felt the popping as joints moved in and out of place, as my ribs cracked and expanded, and as my legs and arms elongated. I was thankful I could no longer hear my own cries.

I was on my hands and knees, thinking that the worst was behind me—pleading to a god I didn't even believe in for this to be over—when my neck spasmed and twisted. Uncontrollably, I thrust my chin frontward and my jaw, as if being ripped from my face, stretched forward. I could taste the familiar sweetness of my own blood as my jaw contorted, and my teeth multiplied and elongated to fill the expanding jaw line. There was another loud pop, followed by desperate cries that I suddenly realized were my own.

Just try to relax. Ash's words came back to me. I hadn't thought they were relevant then, while he was choking me, and I didn't think they were relevant now either. Nonetheless, I tried. I attempted to relax through the pain, to calm my breathing, and slow down my heartrate. I decided to use the gifts I had been given as a vampire to separate myself from the pain my beast was inflicting on me.

"Wolf," Haden shouted excitedly. "I knew it."

His voice was so crisp—clear.

"I'll call Calliope, and she can inform Remy. He'll want to know," William said, without even glancing up.

"You do that," Haden said with a laugh. "I'm calling Iris." Then he added, "Brownie points."

"Dude, I still don't see what you hope to get out of that. Tigers and wolves don't mix, man."

Hmmm, Haden likes Iris.

I arched my back, stretching out as far as possible. It felt good. Then there was a sharp pain, like a knife being thrust into my lower back, as my spinal cord straightened then elongated, ripping through my skin and extending into a tail. I could feel new muscle developing, skin forming, and soft brown fur growing—spreading all around it. It's weird, hard to describe, the way a new body part feels as its growing. It's different than anything else I've ever felt. It's the worst pain I've ever felt, and yet, at the core, there is something comforting—freeing—in the experience.

Long claws slowly began to push out of the tips of my fingers. They looked and felt like knives slicing through the muscles and then the skin of my fingertips. I pressed my face against the bars between Merick and me, and our eyes met. I called out to him, but all that came out was a loud roar before my throat seized up, and another wave of pain took my breath away.

I was hungry, desperately hungry, in a way I've never felt before. I pushed away from the bars, afraid of what I might do if Merick came any closer. Not that I could have broken through the bars—or maybe I could have, I'm not sure. I curled up on the cold hard ground in the corner of my cage. I closed my eyes, waiting—praying for the pain to stop.

Then it did.

When I stood up and opened my eyes, the world seemed different somehow. Maybe it was the

fact that I saw it from only three feet off the ground.
Maybe my wolf just had a different perspective than I
did. Either way, it was clear. I could no longer deny
the fact that I was different.

I was *the one*.

I paced the length of my cage, rubbing my
back against the cold, hard bars. It felt good, but I
knew it would feel even better to be out of the cage
and running free.

Then from somewhere in the distance I heard
the sirens again. William rushed back into the room
and called for Haden to come with him. I wasn't sure
how long they would be gone so I knew I had to take
advantage of their absence while I could.

27

Crouching down on the floor, I closed my eyes and focused on Ciara: her red hair, and bright blue eyes. Her screams are what greeted me when I opened my eyes back up. I hadn't thought about the fact that I might astral project my animal form instead of my human form.

She was standing pressed up against one corner of the room farthest from me, along with Isaac, Jabari, and a couple others. I was lying in the little nest of blankets I had laid out earlier. All of them were watching me closely, ready to lunge if I made any sudden moves.

I started to stand, slowly, but Ciara's screams got louder, so I lay back down again. I tried to tell them that it was only me, but nothing was getting through. I closed my eyes and focused on my human form, trying to change what they saw, but it didn't work. Eventually, I gave up and lunged at a girl with chocolate skin and long black braids who was standing close to me. Because I wasn't a corporeal form it was easy to merge with her form and take over. I had had practice with Ciara, and it seems that it's just as easy with someone you don't know.

"It's just me," I said, breathing hard and holding my hands up to let them know I wasn't going to hurt anyone. "A... Zelina... whatever."

"A?" Ciara said, looking down at the pile of pillows and blankets and then back up at me.

"Yes. I'm sorry, I didn't know any other way to let you know what had happened."

"How did you...? What did happen? Where did you go? It was like, you were here and then you weren't." She was rambling, something she hardly ever did unless she was really distressed. I hated that I was the one distressing her now, but there was nothing I could do about that.

"They've got me and all the other lycanthropes locked up in the holding cells. I'll be there for the next three days. I'm sorry about just disappearing, but I can explain all that later. I wanted to be here, I really—"

"We'll keep her safe," Isaac said.

"Seriously, I'm good," Ciara said, and she really did seem better. Like she had had her first real, peaceful sleep in weeks. "I'm good, as long as you're OK. You are OK, right?"

"Yeah, I'm fine. Why?"

"Oh, I don't know." She rolled her eyes. "Maybe because you came in here looking all furry and mean."

"Yeah, that. Sorry about that. I'm trying not to think about that right now. But I probably should get back before someone realizes I'm gone." Out of habit, I looked down at my wrist, or the borrowed wrist of the woman I had jumped into, but of course there was no monitor there. "Listen, I'll try to come back. I know the sirens just started up again, but I'm not sure why. Make sure you stay low, keep off the streets for a while, and whatever you do, don't come back into the sector. Not yet. I've already worked out a deal with Remy." I glanced across at Isaac and Jabari, who were listening closely. I included them more directly in my instructions. "Remy's going to let her back in, no punishment, but he can't stop the hunt. That means I need to be the one to bring her in. You'll protect her until I can get back, right?"

"We will," Isaac and Jabari answered together.

"But—" Ciara started.

"You just need to hang tight for a few days," I said. Once the moon cycle is over I'll be back to get you. I promise."

I pushed myself out of the borrowed body, and could feel her swinging her arm as if to lash out. "What the hell, man? What *was* that?"

"Long story," someone said, as I faded away.

Opening my eyes, I found myself back on the floor of my temporary living quarters. *Ah, home sweet home.* It was perfect timing, too, because just then the door opened and William and Haden were making their way back to their spots outside my cage.

28

"Merick?" He was pacing the length of his cage, as were all the others. *"Merick, can you hear me?"*

The wolf in the cage next to me growled. I wasn't sure if Merick was still in there, or if maybe he just didn't have any control over his wolf yet.

I slowly made my way to the side of my cage that I shared with M.

"What do you think she's doing?" William asked.

"Beats me," Haden answered as he shrugged and leaned forward in his chair. Watching me. I could feel it—hear it—as clearly as if he had announced it to the room. My hearing was keen, crisp, clear. I could hear every movement in the room around me. Without even looking, I knew where everyone was and what they were doing. I could understand the differences in the sounds their paws made on the hard concrete floor. I could distinguish each individual heartbeat; even the small changes in breathing patterns didn't escape me.

I narrowed my focus. Eyes and ears on Merick, I let out a loud, thundering roar. Merick fell to the ground, his body thrashing, transforming—a single scream escaping his lips. When the change was complete, he was there, naked, lying on the cold cement floor, Merick once again. His heartrate was unusual—dangerously slow.

"What the hell?" William quickly stood up, kicking his chair over in the process. "What just happened?"

"She commanded him. She commanded his change."

I did what? I think I was as shocked and scared as William.

"I need to let the Council know," Haden said, as he raced to the door. "Holy shit." He came to a quick halt at the end of the row of cages.

"What now?" William asked, out of breath, yet breathing heavy as he turned toward Haden's voice.

"It's not just him. The lion changed too."

Sure enough, when I looked over at Hudson's cage, he too was lying, unconscious, on the floor of his cage. I could hear his heartbeat, critically slow in his chest, from across the room. I called out, howling, but the only answer I got back was the nervous grunts, growls, and roars from the other caged animals. All eyes were on me, but I didn't care. At that moment, all I cared about was Merick and Hudson. I needed to know that they were all right.

Haden took a deep breath, headed to the door, and left, leaving William alone in the room with six new, hungry, and confused lycanthropes, and two unconscious young men who were probably going to be terrified when they woke up—if they woke up.

"Yeah...no sure...I'm okay. You go on ahead." William scanned the room. He walked up and down each row, checking all the cage doors, making sure the locks were secure.

It didn't take long before Haden was back, followed by Iris, Remy, Ash, the guard who had brought the others in, a women I recognized from the clinic—a doctor, I suspected—and U, Uma, from my selection class. She had been assigned as a caregiver—a medical assistant. Why they would bring her here I had no idea, and, from the look on her face, neither did she. She looked terrified.

The guard and the doctor, a tall, dark-haired woman with delicate features, made their way into Haden's cage as the others came around to Merick's.

"Uma, do you plan to assist me from out there?" the woman asked.

Uma just stood there, gripping the bars of the cage. "No, sorry Amelia, I didn't mean—"

Amelia? She's a first-born. *First-borns* are rare because, for whatever reason, it is uncommon that a first-born actually survives birth. You're considered a first-born if you are the first child born in the year. All first-borns are given an 'A' indicator, and later, after Selection Week, are allowed to choose a name that begins with the letter A. I was the first-born of my class. My choice of a name is another story. I've never actually met another first-born. Councilman Ash, although his name begins with A, was born and turned long before the sectors were even established, so he doesn't count.

"Then come in, please," Amelia said.

Amelia bent down to examine Haden, reaching up for Uma to hand her a medical bag. After what seemed like hours, but was probably only mere minutes, she looked up and called across the room, "He'll be fine." Her voice was soft yet it carried through the room with ease. "The forced change may have caused some muscle strain, and I believe he has a broken rib, maybe two, but other than that it didn't hurt him. He should be able to heal during the hibernation stage." She continued the report of her examination. "All vitals seem to be in check. We'll need to make sure he eats as soon as he wakes up, but other than that he should be as good as new by tomorrow's nightfall."

"Good," Councilman Cruz said, as he walked through the door. Remy, Iris, and Ash quickly turned their attention to him as he made his way down the row to stand before them. "To what do I owe the pleasure of your visit? Was it concern for my young shifters, or just mere curiosity about what might happen to the girl?"

"As the leader of the sector, they are my shifters as well," Remy replied, taking a step forward. "When I heard what had happened, like you, I wanted to make sure no one was harmed. As for the girl, it is clear that there is more we must learn."

"Learn? You mean to study her?"

Remy turned back to Merick's cage, watching as the guard opened the lock, and escorted Amelia and Uma in. "I mean to study them both."

Silence filled the room as everyone watched—waited.

Uma peered through the bars of Merick's cage and locked her gaze on me. I couldn't tell if she knew who I was, or if she was just fascinated by being so close to a wolf.

"His heartrate is already improving. His transformation was less damaging to his system than the other boy's," Amelia said, as she stood up, handed her medical bag to Uma, and moved to leave the cage.

Ash watched closely from just outside Merick's cage. "I have been around far too long, and seen more than my fair share of things, but this..." he said, shaking his head, "...how is this even possible?"

"As far as I know, it isn't," Amelia answered. "Only an alpha can command a change and then only on their pack members. Zelina is too young. Besides, wasn't he the one who infected her, and not the other way around?"

"He was," Cruz answered, before Ash had a chance.

"Then it shouldn't be..."

"What about the other one? The lion?" Remy interrupted. "Zelina has no connection to his bloodline. She was infected with Teagan's blood, not his."

"I don't know."

Remy glared at me through the bars. "She's wolf. Is she more?"

He wasn't asking me, but the lion inside of me roared out in response. I could feel my body shifting and my muscles adjusting, fighting to stay in their current form. If I had thought prayer would help, I would have prayed not to change again. The fight didn't last long.

"What's happening?" William asked, leaning closer to Haden.

"She's changing, again," Haden said in a near whisper.

"This can't be happening," Amelia said.

Whether it could or couldn't be happening didn't matter because he was right. Suddenly I was there, on my hands and knees, kneeling before them, all of them. I looked up and I could see the shock on their faces. The transformation back to human form hadn't been nearly as painful as my first transformation, but that didn't mean I wasn't sore. I stood up, stretched, and then crossed to the bars that separated us. I should have been embarrassed, standing there naked before them, but I wasn't. My hands were trembling, and my body was covered with a thick, transparent gel, from the sudden change, but other than that and a little muscle cramping, I felt fine. I gripped the bars in front of me and leaned in. "I'm hungry," was all I said. No one answered.

29

Amelia rushed to my cage. "You need to let me examine her." Turning to the guard, she reached out, "Unlock the cage or give me your keys so I can do it myself." She wasn't afraid, and a piece of me respected her for that.

"It's too dangerous," Cruz responded, holding the guard back. "She shouldn't even be awake right now. It should take years before she's able to come out of a transformation without hibernating. We don't know what else she is capable of."

"I don't care," Amelia pleaded. "Please."

"And if she shifts again?"

"I've been a lycanthrope for sixty-two years now. I believe I can handle myself."

Sixty-two years? I thought. She doesn't look a day over thirty. I knew the lycanthropy virus slowed the aging process, but I had no idea it slowed it that much.

They stood there, face-to-face in silence, until finally Remy reached out to the guard. "Give me the keys, I'll go in with her."

"You?" Cruz asked.

"Yes, me. She is my vampire and I will not fear her." He took the keys and unlocked the cage door.

As he stepped inside our eyes met. I knew what he wanted to know. He was curious if I could shift again so soon, and, if so, what would I be? I even knew why he wanted—needed—to know, and I was all right with it. Deep down, I even understood why he wanted it so much, even if I didn't agree with him entirely. However, my body was tired, and I wasn't going to put myself through the pain just to please him.

Amelia stepped into the cage and motioned to the blanket curled up in the corner. "Do you mind sitting?"

"No." I picked up the blanket and sat down. The bench was cold—hard—but it didn't matter. Being off my feet felt wonderful at that moment. I leaned back against the wall and wrapped the thin blue blanket around me.

"Are you cold?"

"A little."

She placed her hand on my forehead, and I recoiled from the heat of it. "You're freezing."

I am a vampire, I thought to myself.

She looked back through the bars of the cage, and motioned for Uma to bring her bag. She did.

"Are you OK?" Uma whispered as she came into the cage.

I nodded.

She smiled.

Amelia checked my temperature, and began her report. "Her temperature is unusually low for a lycanthrope, not only for after a transformation but, in general." She continued her examination.

"Well, I guess maybe that's because I'm not your typical lycanthrope."

"No, I suppose you're not." She didn't seem nervous or scared. From the way she looked at me, watching my every move and examining me so thoroughly, I would say she was intrigued. She had the same look in her eyes that Ash gets when I surprise him.

"I'm not going to attack her you know," I told Remy, as he watched me over Amelia's shoulder.

"I didn't think you would.

"Although..." I started. Remy just looked at me, which didn't surprise me.

It was Amelia who asked, "Although?"

"Although, I am still hungry. Do you think I could get something to drink?" Out of the corner of my eye, I saw Ash literally flash out of the room then back in. It had to be less than a second, but when he returned he was holding a bottle out in front of me. "Thank you." I took a sip, and I could feel the hunger fading away.

"It's amazing," Amelia muttered to herself.

"What is?" Both Remy and Cruz asked at the same time, as Cruz made his way into the cage to stand next to Remy.

Amelia summarized her findings. "She's perfectly healthy. Not a single broken bone or fracture. Not even a bruise to mention. You would think there would be some sign of her transformation, but other than appearing to be a little tired, there isn't—not one."

"Can you explain it?" Remy asked, hopefully.

She just shook her head. I wasn't surprised that she couldn't explain it, but I was disappointed. I had hoped Amelia—the doctor—would at least be able to explain who or what I am.

"Maybe…maybe it's the vampire virus," Amelia continued. "I'm not sure. I'd like to do more blood work, to see if the lycanthrope virus is more predominate now that she's shifted. It would also be good if…" She was looking at me now, waiting, but I didn't know what for.

"It would be good if what?" I asked, not knowing if I wanted to hear the answer.

"If I could get a blood sample while you're in your animal form." She never once took her eyes off of me.

"I…I don't think I have any control over that. I…" I looked around, but no one else seemed to have an answer either.

"No matter. Maybe in time." She finished her examination a few minutes later, thanked me, and left. Uma gathered up all of the medical supplies into the bag and followed her out. Not another word was said until they, and the guards, were gone.

"I wish to speak to the girl alone," Remy said to no one—everyone—but no one moved. "Now."

"What about the other…?" William started to ask.

"They won't be an issue," Cruz answered. "The two boys are unconscious and won't be waking up any time soon. The others have shifted. It will be months before they are able to retain any memories after a shift."

It will be months before they are able to retain any memories after a shift? What does that mean? I filed that little piece of information away in the back of my mind. I needed to remember to ask Iris about it later.

William looked back at Haden, who just nodded his confirmation. That was good enough for him, and he began to exit, followed by Haden and Iris. Ash stayed behind, waiting—for what, I wasn't sure. Permission to leave? Maybe.

Cruz stepped forward, "I don't feel right, leaving you unprotected. Maybe I should—"

"I'll be fine," Remy assured him. They stood there like children in the middle of a staring contest—neither one wanting to back down, but eventually Cruz conceded. He turned and made his way to the exit, stopping only briefly to glance back—at me.

"You may go too," Remy instructed. Ash nodded, turned, and followed Cruz out.

The door echoed behind them, and once again, only for a brief moment, the silence seemed to fill the air around me. "You are—"

"Intriguing, I know."

"I was going to say, special."

"What?" Special was not at all how I felt. Different. Weird. Strange. Odd. All those words seemed to fit, but special? No, I hadn't thought of myself as special. Not then, or ever in my past as far back as I could remember.

Remy pulled Haden's chair into my cage and sat down. "You are. You're special. You might not realize it, yet, but in time you'll come to realize that what you have, what you are, is a gift."

I could remember, like it was yesterday, how he had stood on that stage presenting me to the rest of the sector residents. How he had made me feel like

I was nothing, like I was insignificant. He had painted me as a monster—not a vampire, not a wolf, not a lion—but an abomination of all three.

"Why now? Why are you so intrigued by me now, when only weeks ago you were considering barring me from the sector and exiling me out into the wastelands?"

"I never honestly considered that as an option. Not really. I knew at the time—as I know now—how important you are to the future of our society. But, as the leader, it is my duty, my responsibility, to follow the rules—the laws that we have developed within the sector, and those placed upon us by the Governing Council."

"Even the ones you don't believe in?"

"They were set up for a reason. I believed in them at one time. Now..." He leaned back and closed his eyes. "*Now* I know that if we are to survive then we must make sacrifices. We must make changes." When he opened his eyes, there was something fierce in them. Something passionate. "Zelina, you are the key to our survival. It won't be an easy task, and many will hate you for the changes you bring, but there are many of us who will stand behind you, support you, even fight for you."

"You? You're going to stand behind me— support me?" He didn't answer, and I wasn't surprised. "How will you fight for me when you have to be *the leader* and follow the sector laws?"

"It will take time for us to study—to learn what you really are and how you are even able to exist. But if you work *with* us, not against us, then when the time is right I will fight for you—with you."

"And when you do learn what I really am and how all this works, what then? You'll use my blood to make everyone in Sector C...what did Iris call me? A hybrid? Is that what you want, for everyone to be the same?"

"I believe that if we are united as one race we can end the fighting, stop the inevitable extinction of our societies, and prevent the few remaining sectors from closing down."

I couldn't believe what I was hearing, nor did I believe he was right, but if I wanted to protect my friend then I had to play along.

"You already know what you need to do if you want me to work with you."

"I do, and you have my word."

It was as close to a commitment as I was going to get from him. That didn't mean I was going to trust him. We wouldn't be singing *Kumbaya* around a campfire together anytime soon, and I wasn't *drinking the kool-aid,* as M says.

"So what happens next?" I asked.

"Nothing. You remain here, under the protection of William and Haden. Once the moon cycle is complete, you'll be let out with all the others. Life will continue as it has been. Word of your transformation will be released, but any information concerning the forced change you commanded from Merick and Hudson will be kept confidential until we know more."

"How? How will it be kept confidential when so many people already know?" I wanted to ask how he expected to keep Merick and Hudson quiet, and all the other new lycanthropes, but I didn't.

217

He smiled, "The others listen to me. As for your friends, Merick and Hudson, they won't remember it ever happening, and neither will the other young shifters." He stood up. "But you remember, don't you?"

"I remember everything."

"Hmmm. That's a shame. I've been told the pain is excruciating, and that forgetting is the only thing that makes it bearable."

"It is. Excruciating," I said. I wanted more detail—more information about why I could remember but the others couldn't. But I bit my tongue. I'd wait till I could talk to Iris.

Remy stood up, carried his chair out of my cell, then shut and locked the door behind him. "I'll have someone bring you something to eat. I'm sure you're still hungry." Then he turned to leave. Before he made it all the way to the door, he stopped and looked back over his shoulder. "If you do decide to shift again this moon cycle, maybe try for a lion this time." He smiled then left.

Decide.

Try.

He makes it sound like I'm in control.

Maybe I am.

30

I sat in the cell for a few more hours, watching the others pace along the sides of their cages, and listening as their growls, roars, and howls echoed through the room. I felt trapped. I needed to find a way out, a way to help Ciara and the others. I wanted desperately to talk to Merick, to figure out what my next move should be, but he was lying unconscious on the floor of his cage with no sign of when he would wake up.

Remy had done what he said he would, and sent food to me, but it was only a plate of raw steak and a small glass of blood. I needed more. I guess I should have been thankful that they allowed me to eat off of a plate since the others had raw meat tossed into their cages and were left to eat straight off the dirty floor. I wasn't so sure that when they woke up they would like that too much. Then again, maybe they really wouldn't even remember.

I was still hungry. "I don't suppose you could get me something else to eat, or maybe someone to drink?"

Haden glared at me through the bars of my cage. "Someone?"

Good, it didn't go unheard.

"That's what I said."

"I don't think the boss would allow a donor in here, especially at night."

I glanced down at my wrist. My internal monitor read 11:21. "It's almost midnight; that's practically morning." He didn't respond. I looked around and saw that most of the others had fallen asleep or had finally settled down. "Shouldn't they all be shifting back by now? Shouldn't Merick and Hudson have woken up by now?"

"No and yes." Haden's answer wasn't really an answer. "Why aren't you sleeping?"

I stood up, crossing to the bars of my cage separating me from them. William just watched, he looked tired, but Haden…he was on guard. "I'm not tired." In all honesty, I was, but I didn't want to be sleeping when M finally woke up. "And what kind of answer is *No and yes*? Explain."

"No, they shouldn't have shifted back by now. Nor should you have. A young shifter stays in their animal form through the moon cycle, until *they* can learn to control their transformations instead of having the moon cycle control it for them. Yes, the wolf and the lion should have woken up by now. They weren't in their animal forms very long. Thus, they shouldn't have needed this long of a hibernation period. Typically, during the first few years a shifter will hibernate for a quarter of the time they spent in their animal form. It can be longer for new shifters, but not this long."

Haden was throwing too much information at me all at once, but I was desperate to understand. If Merick and Hudson had been in animal form for…I don't *know* how long. The pain had been so intense, I had no idea how much time had passed. Besides, I wasn't sure how long I had been gone—visiting with Ciara and the others. "How long? How long were they in their animal forms? How long did it take me to shift? It felt like hours, but—"

"It was only—" William started to answer, but Haden quickly stopped him.

"Don't." They exchanged glances, but didn't say anything else. It was as if they were having an entire conversation without saying a word.

"Don't what? Don't tell me? Why? Why can't you tell me? Is it because you think I've done something wrong? Is it because you're afraid? Why won't you…?"

"It's because they are watching." His voice was low, almost a whisper, and he didn't move a muscle as he spoke.

I glanced up. Sure enough the familiar blinking red lights were scattered across the ceiling. "Of course they are, why wouldn't they be, but what does that matter? Considering all the information you were just throwing at me, what's wrong with telling me how long it took me to shift, or how long I was in my animal form?"

"Because I was giving you textbook information. Stuff you should have learned in your classes. New shifters aren't supposed to remember their first shift, second shift, hell, even their third or fourth. There is something seriously wrong with you that yo—"

"Hey." William cut him off. "There is no need for that. Just leave her alone."

I pressed my back against the wall and slid to the floor. "Since you can't tell me anything, can you at least bring me something to eat?" I added a smile for good measure.

"Fine." Haden got up and made his way out, leaving William and me alone, or as alone as two people can be in a room full of hungry beasts and sleeping lycanthropes.

I had hoped he would share some meaningful insight, words of encouragement, something...anything. No such luck. All he said, after the door shut behind Haden was, "I'm on your side. Haden... well, he's a good guy. He'll come around."

"Yeah, that's what I hear."

"What?" he asked.

Crap, did I say that out loud? "No, nothing. Just talking to myself."

"Just keep your chin up."

Easier said than done, but I'll take it, I thought to myself. Out loud I said, "Thank you, for being on my side. I think I might need it."

He just nodded.

31

Shortly after Haden left, the door creaked open. "That didn't take long..." William started to say, as he looked back over his shoulder, but it wasn't Haden who came through the door. "Oh, hey Amelia. What's up?"

"Nothing, I just needed to check up on the patients," she said, as she made her way back to my cage, peeking in on Hudson and Merick as she passed.

"They're both still sleeping, but I'm guessing you already knew that," William said. "What's really going on? What's in the bag?" he asked, nodding down at a brown paper bag she was clutching close to her chest.

"Just a change of clothes, for Zelina. Can I have a minute in private with her please?" She nodded toward my cage, but didn't actually look at me.

"You know I can't do that..."

"William, it's important, and I promise it won't take long. Just give me..." She glanced down at her internal monitor. "Give me five minutes, please."

William stood up. "Five minutes, that's it."

"Perfect. Thank you." She watched as he made his way to the door. After it closed behind him, she turned toward my cage. "I've brought you a change of clothes," she said, reaching through the bars of my cage to hand me the bag.

"Thank you."

"I wanted to properly introduce myself. My name is Amelia. As you know, I'm a doctor at the sector clinic."

I reached out through the bars and shook her hand. She was warm—hot even—like all lycanthropes. "I'm Zelina."

"I know who you are. We all do."

"You all do?" I asked, as I pulled the clothes out of the bag and started to dress. The gooey substance that had coated my skin after my last transformation had more or less dried up and flaked off. The clothes felt soft and clean, the way new clothes always do.

"When a first-born survives, everyone in the sector takes notice. I've been watching you since…well, honestly, since before you were born."

Since before I was born? OK, that's a little creepy. "Why?" I asked.

"There were three of you, all expected to be delivered—" She glanced up at the cameras "—on the same day," she finished in a whisper.

It wasn't like it was some big secret. "Right," I agreed. "Me, Ciara, and a boy. He didn't make it."

"That's right." She sat down just outside of the cage. "Before you and C53—"

"Ciara," I corrected her. We had earned our names, and even if Ciara wasn't there to claim it, I'd do it for her.

"Ciara, sorry. Before you and Ciara, there hadn't been two selection students born on the same day in over two hundred years, and even back then they hardly ever survived." She leaned in close, "The fact that you both survived... It wasn't just a coincidence."

"What do you mean?"

"Right from the beginning of the pregnancy, that first time I heard your heartbeat, I knew there was something different about you."

"Why me?"

"You had a strong heartbeat. Stronger and faster than the others. Plus, your breeder, she was special. Even she knew you would be the first-born. She knew early on. She said she could feel you inside of her long before she should have been able to."

"My breeder? You knew her?"

"Of course, very well," Amelia said, smiling. "When she was pregnant, she dreamed about you. She used to tell me how you would be born with the most beautiful chestnut hair and bronze eyes. A striking beauty, the kind you only read about, she used to say."

She dreamed about me? I wondered if her dreams were really premonitions. *Did I get my visions from my breeder—my mother?*

"Do I look like her?"

"No. You have her stature and her majestic calm, but she was fairer of skin than you, and had fiery red hair." She laughed. "You know, now that I

225

think about it, you are actually her only born who didn't get the fiery red hair."

Fiery red hair? My first thought was of C. Ciara has always had the most beautiful red hair. Carrot Top, our classmates had called her. I knew that nickname was a source of insecurity for her, or maybe it was just the fact that her hair was different, but I had always admired C's hair. I opened my mouth to ask her more about this woman—my breeder—but she was already continuing.

"Even now, when she talks about your birth, you can see her fill up with pride. It's a great honor to deliver a first-born."

"But that was seventeen years ago. I thought that..." As a Council liaison I had access to information other sector members didn't have. I knew that being a breeder was a short-term assignment, and that after you're no longer useful you're either killed or banished.

"Yes, typically, breeders are only kept active for eight years. That is what you're thinking, is it not?"

"It is."

"The only thing I can say is, she was different. She was an active breeder for thirteen years. In all that time she only lost one birth, and she had twelve live births—two of which were born after your selection class."

I thought back on the kids in the two selection classes right behind mine. I could picture only two, out of all the kids, who actually had red hair. *Wow, they must be my little brothers,* I thought. *Can I even call them that?*

"But the sector laws say that breeders are released from their positions after six births."

"I know. As I said, she was different. Her infants were strong, active—they were survivors. She was the best breeder we had, and the Council didn't want to lose her."

"So what happened to her? Where is she now?" I was pretty sure I already knew the answer. The sector laws say that when a breeder is released from their duties they will be given the option of becoming a donor or defecting to live in the wastelands as a castaway. Since Amelia had just told me she still knew her, she had to be a donor. I wondered why she had chosen that life.

"The vampires turned her."

"What?" That wasn't the answer I had expected.

"It didn't happen right away. In fact, it was only recently that she was turned. After she was released from her position as a breeder, she chose to stay in the sector as a donor. She served as a donor for fifteen years, until—"

"Fifteen years? Donors don't—wait, that means she was just turned. As in, this year."

"That's right."

"Why? What made them decide to turn her now? How did it even happen? Who did it?" I wasn't sure why I even cared, but for some reason I needed to know.

"Councilman Remy did it. They couldn't use the injection because she was too old. She turned forty-six earlier this year, and until then the most elderly person we had given the injection to without complications had been thirty-two. He didn't want to risk something happening to her, so he turned her himself."

"You mean?"

"Yes, through the exchange of blood. It's dangerous, I know, but he felt that finding a way to keep her was worth the risk."

I hadn't heard of anyone being turned through the old method in almost three hundred years. Why he would attempt it now, I had no idea. So I asked. "Why did he…?"

"Because of you. She followed your life. You were a first-born—you're special. When she found out that you had survived, it was a source of pride for her. Then, after she was no longer needed as a breeder, she chose to stay in the sector as a donor so that she could watch you grow up. After she found out what happened during Selection Week, the fact that you had been infected with both the vampire virus and the lycanthropy virus, she asked to be turned. The Council was against it, even Remy had his reservations, but…"

"But what?" I asked.

"But somehow she changed his mind. Eventually, he said yes. I think he thought that turning her might give him leverage to get you to help us if you fought us."

"Leverage, nice." *So typical.* "So who is she? Can I meet her?"

"I…"

"If she's supposed to be his leverage, I have to at least meet her before Remy can use her to get what he wants from me. Besides, you wouldn't have told me all of this if you hadn't already intended to let us meet."

"I'm not really sure what I *intended*, but she is my friend, and I know she would like to meet you as well." She reached through the bars and took my hand. "I'll have to talk to Remy first before I can set anything up."

"That's fine. I've got all the time in the world." I glanced back at my little cage. "I'm not going anywhere."

"No, I don't suppose you are."

"Time's up," William announced as he pushed the door open.

Amelia stood up, and when she released my hand, there was a small folded piece of paper there. I palmed it, moving to the back of my cage where I could read it under my blanket, hidden from the camera's view, and William's.

> A ~ You'll never believe what I've discovered. We need to talk. This is huge. ~ U
>
> P.S. Good luck with the moon cycle. You've got a lot of people rooting for you out here.

My mind was going a mile a minute, wondering what Uma could have learned. She had been working with Amelia in the clinic and apparently trusted the doctor enough to deliver her message, but what it all meant I had no way to know.

32

I managed to fall asleep for a few hours, but was woken up by the sound of the alarms coming through the door as William and Haden headed out. "She's out. She isn't going to be waking up for at least another couple of hours," Haden said. "Besides, if she does wake up the guards will see it on the monitors and send someone in."

I stayed curled up under my blanket and out of sight. With them gone, it was the perfect time for me to reach out to Ciara again, but I had to make sure I didn't draw any attention to myself. Making sure every part of me was covered, I closed my eyes and pictured the dark basement room, the dusty couches, and the pile of pillows and blankets in the corner. When I opened my eyes I was there, but something was different. I was surrounded by complete silence, I couldn't even hear the others down the hall talking and playing cards. I walked down the hall, checking behind every door, but no one was around.

"Ciara?" I called out.

Nothing.

"Isaac? Jabari?"

I started running, unsure of where I should go until I saw a stairwell up ahead. I ran up the stairs two at a time and burst through the door when I made it to the top. The empty lobby greeted me with an uneasy stillness. A shiver ran through my body, and I almost screamed out. Almost. When I turned there was a small girl standing in the corner. She couldn't have been older than five or six. Her hair was a vibrant red and down to her bottom. She was wearing a bright yellow dress with a white flower pattern and strappy white sandals. Something felt so familiar about her, but I couldn't place why. I knew I had never seen her before—we don't dress like that in Sector C—but there was a feeling in my gut that didn't seem right.

"Are you all alone?" I asked.

She just shook her head.

"Are you OK?"

She shook her head again, but still didn't speak.

"Do you need help?"

Without answering she turned and started running down a long hallway off to her right. I quickly followed. It felt like I was running through a maze of hallways. White walls and dusty windows surrounded me, but the farther we got the cleaner and brighter it became. I could hear noises in the distance, but didn't see anyone.

When I turned a corner at the end of the hall, I stopped. I felt like I had run into a wall. There were people all around me, crowding the hallway, rushing in and out of different rooms, and talking in little groups. I couldn't see the little girl in the yellow dress anymore, but I was sure she had gone that way—I had seen her turn the corner. No one looked at me or even said anything as I made my way through the crowd and down the hall.

There, at the far end of the hall, was a woman with long red hair, sitting with her face in her hands. It was faint, but I could hear as she struggled to breathe through the tears. Her heart was racing in her chest, and as she looked up our eyes met, only for a second. I blinked and I was back in my cage, breathing heavy, and my face was wet from tears I hadn't even known I had shed.

33

It wasn't until noon the next day that Merick finally woke up. I was sitting in my cage with my forehead against the bars, my hands stretched out through them holding a hand full of cards.

"It's your turn," Haden said. "Been your turn for about five minutes now. You've taken so long William's gone and fallen asleep, again."

It was true, William was sleeping, again. I couldn't really blame him though, it had been a long night and none of us had gotten much sleep since we arrived the previous day, and what little sleep we had managed hadn't been good.

"Yeah, I get it. I'm thinking." He only had two cards in his hand, and I still had four. If I didn't play this hand right, I was going to lose, and I hate losing.

I lost.

"Ha. Not so tough after all are you?" He was kidding of course. It was, after all, just a card game.

"What are you playing?" His voice was harsh, raspy, and quiet, but I didn't have to turn around to know it was Merick.

I jumped up, dropping the rest of my cards to the floor, and rushed to the side of his cage. "M. Oh my stars M, you're awake." I reached through the bars, but he didn't move.

"Yeah, I think so." He was still lying down, rubbing his head, but his eyes were open, and he was looking my way. He smiled.

Oh my word, that smile.

"You OK?"

"Yeah, a little headache, but I'm good." It took him a few minutes to finally sit up. "What's going on with all of them?" He was staring around at our former classmates, who, except for Hudson, were all still in their animal forms—some pacing in their cages but most fast asleep.

"What do you mean?" Yup, stupid question, but I didn't know what else to say.

"You know what I mean. Why haven't they changed back yet?"

"More like why did you," Haden mumbled under his breath. I think he was talking to himself. He wasn't even looking at us, but *hello* we're all lycanthropes here. We all have incredible hearing.

"Excuse me?" M said.

It wasn't a question, not really, but I felt he deserved an answer. "You kinda changed back early. You and Hudson actually."

"What do you mean we changed back early? The moon cycle's not over yet?"

"Over? It's only been one night."

"One night? I thought lycanthropes aren't supposed to transform out of their animal form at all during their first few moon cycles," he said. Apparently he knew a lot more about this stuff than I did.

Did I miss that day in class? I wondered, knowing full well I had never missed a day of class.

"They're not." I looked over at Haden, who clearly wanted me to shut up, but he didn't say anything so I continued. "Not until they can learn to control their transformations. At least, that's what Haden tells me," I added with a little smile back at my *favorite* babysitter.

"But if it's only been one night..." Merick smiled. "Wait, does that mean—what? Hudson and I can already control our transformations?" Evidently he took it as a good sign.

"No," Haden answered, before I could. "It takes months for young shifters to control their transformations or to control what they do while they're in their animal form. That's why we use the cages. You've been told all this before."

"If it takes months, why are we already in our human form, huh?" Merick asked. He had a huge smirk plastered on his face.

"Do you remember making a conscious decision to shift back into your human form?" Haden asked.

"I... Well, no, but—"

"I rest my case," Haden said.

"Whatever," Merick said, as he crossed to stand next to me, with only the bars separating us. "What about you?" There was so much eagerness—anticipation—hope—in his voice.

I knew what he was asking, but I wasn't sure how to answer.

"Wolf." Haden had answered before I had the chance. "She's a wolf. That's what you want to know, right? I mean, that's what everyone wants to know."

"Seriously?" M's eyes were wide, and he had an ear to ear smile plastered across his face. "Wait, so you...you were able to transform back early too?"

"Yeah. They think it has something to do with the vampire virus in my blood." I glanced back over my shoulder at Haden, who didn't stop me, but was listening intently. I knew if I said too much he'd jump in and put an end to it.

"The vampire virus?"

"Yeah. They didn't have another explana—" I stopped myself.

Yup, I had said too much.

"But I don't have the vampire virus in my blood..."

Yeah, that isn't entirely true, I thought to myself, but bit my lip so that I didn't say it out loud.

"And neither does Hudson," M said.

Both Haden and I sat there, not knowing what to say. Luckily we didn't have to wait long before the guard pushed open the door and called out, "Lunch time." He came in, dragging a rolling cart full of, you guessed it, raw meat.

"Wonderful. It's so great to see we have such variety in our meals these days," I said. OK, so maybe it was a little sarcastic, but come on, all I've had to eat in the last twenty-four hours has been raw meat and lukewarm blood.

The guard tossed the meat into the cages of anyone who was awake, avoiding those who were still sleeping. Like me, Merick got a plate.

"What is that...?" Merick had the exact same reaction I had the first time.

I took my plate, trying to show him that it would be fine. "Just try not to think about it. It actually doesn't taste bad if you can get over the way it looks, and the texture."

"Yeah, I don't know. Couldn't I get mine medium rare, or at least seared?" he asked, as he held the plate back out to the guard.

"Nope," the guard answered, not even looking back. "You hungry Haden?"

"No man, I'm good. I'll grab something later."

"What about your *friend*?" he asked, as he kicked Williams's foot. "Does he need some nourishment?"

At that, William yawned, stretched, and asked, "Do I smell fresh...?" He opened his eyes. "Oh never mind."

"You want something to drink?" the guard asked, looking down at the half-asleep William.

"Sure, but I don't think we're allowed to have donors in here. That, is unless you're offering."

"Yeah, in your dreams. You need to keep those fangs to yourself, but I can bring you a bottle if you need one."

"Yeah, whatever, thanks." William leaned back and closed his eyes again.

34

The rest of the day was pretty much what I had expected. William and Haden spent their time playing cards. Merick and I talked—out loud for our babysitters and the cameras, but our real conversation was taking place telepathically, just for us. I think I was actually starting to get used to communicating that way.

I finally had a chance to tell him what happened when I astral projected to find Ciara. I think he actually got a little jealous.

'Dude, that's so not fair. You get visions, telepathy, and now astral projection? What are you going to tell me next, you can teleport or something?"

I decided not to tell him about Ash's teleportation abilities, or how I had teleported to Iris's apartment when I thought Ash was about to grab my astral projection. I'd tell him later, when he wasn't already so jealous.

Hudson finally woke up a little before five o'clock, and the guard brought him in some food—raw meat, of course, which didn't seem to bother him as much as it had Merick and me. As if on cue, when Hudson finished, Amelia walked in.

"It's nice to see you boys up and about," Amelia said, nodding to Merick, and motioning to Haden to unlock Hudson's cage. Haden just handed her the keycard. "How are you feeling?" she asked Hudson as she entered.

"Who's she?" M asked.

"Amelia. She's a doctor. Don't worry, she seems nice."

"Good, I feel good," Hudson said. "Maybe a little sore, but nothing too bad." He was standing now, stretching, and I realized he seemed taller now than he had before he shifted.

It has to be my mind playing tricks on me, right?

"That's good. I half expected you to be doubled over in pain from the broken ribs, but it seems you just might be all healed up." She held out her hand smiling, "I'm Amelia, one of the clinic doctors. I just need to do a quick physical and get a small blood sample then I'll be out of your hair. All right?"

"Yeah, sure, OK." Hudson sat down and held out his arm as he leaned back against the bars.

"Don't tell me you're afraid of needles?" she asked, as she ran her hands across his rib cage. I'm sure she was joking, but I think she actually had hit the nail on the head. I could hear as Hudson's heart pounded in his chest and, believe me, I understood.

Hmm, I thought I was the only one around here with a fear of needles, I thought to myself.

"No. I just…"

"Ribs are all healed, like I suspected. Even all the bruises are gone." He still wasn't watching, but I could see her prepping her needle secretly at her side

239

as she examined him. "Just a little longer and—" The needle was in.

"Augh, that—I was not ready for that."

Well, well, well, she's sneaky, and kinda clever. I do like her.

"All done. See, it wasn't so bad was it?" She was smiling as she packed up her bag and pulled the cage door shut behind her.

I was watching Hudson. He didn't answer, and his heart was still pounding as he rubbed his arm where she had just poked him. "Hey H, you OK?"

Nothing.

"H? You all right over there?" His heartbeat got louder and louder, and I could smell the sweat that had started to appear at the nape of his neck and around his forehead. "I think there's something wrong with…"

"Not to worry," Amelia said. "He's just shifting. It's perfectly normal. Sometimes strong emotions such as pain, fear, or anger can activate a lycanthrope's shift during the moon cycle. Besides, he shouldn't have transformed back yet anyway. It's best if he completes the moon cycle in transformation."

She was right, he was shifting. It didn't take long before he was on his hands and knees and his muscles began to shift. The screams came next. I would have given anything to be anywhere but there.

"Did I…? Did that…?"

I looked over at M, and he was gripping the bars of his cage so hard his knuckles were turning white, and he was staring at Hudson.

"You really don't remember anything about your transformation, do you?"

"No."

That one little word said it all. It was sad. He was scared, and I almost felt sorry for him, but I *did* remember my transformation—the pain, the sound of my own screams echoing in my ears—and honestly, I think I would rather have forgotten.

"Your turn," Amelia said, as she approached M's cage.

She reached for the lock, but M quickly grabbed it, blocking her access. "Yeah, I don't think I really want to do that again right now…or really ever."

She laughed. "You do know that not giving a blood sample isn't going to stop the transformation. It's a full moon tonight; whether you shift now or later, it doesn't really matter to me. Besides…" she leaned in, whispering, "…you're a tough guy, I don't think a little needle could scare you into shifting. What do you say, how about you let me in so I can finish my job?"

Merick was only half listening, as he continued to watch Hudson's every move. Hudson was almost halfway done with his shifting, but still crying out in agony. Merick turned to me, and his eyes were glossed over.

"You got this, M. I promise, you can handle it. It doesn't last long."

"I got this."

It wasn't a question, but I answered anyway, *"Yeah."*

He looked back at Amelia who nodded down to his hand, still covering the lock. She was still smiling kindly. "Don't worry, I promise when you shift back you won't remember any of it."

I still wasn't so sure if that was a good thing or a bad thing, I guess time would tell.

M stepped back, letting Amelia into the cage. She drew his blood sample then stepped out, pulling the cage door shut behind her.

We all waited. Even Haden and William had stopped playing whatever card game they had been playing and watched.

"See, you handled it like a pro. No shifting." She turned, making her way past my cage. "Hello Zelina."

"Hello." I wanted to stop her, ask her if she had talked to Remy about me meeting my breeder, or at least find out if I could talk to Uma—if I could see her and learn what she had found out—but I didn't. It wasn't the right time.

"Want to give a sample?" she asked, smiling.

"Do I have to?"

"No. I think I have enough of your vamp blood."

"My vamp blood?"

"When you're in human form the vampire virus seems to be dominant. Although, I have a theory. I think when you shift the lycanthrope virus will become dominant. So, I'd love to get another sample after you shift again. If you wouldn't mind, that is."

"Yeah, I'm not so sure that's going to—"

"It'll happen, trust me. Even your last sample had a little more active lycanthropy in it than your previous samples," she said.

She seemed happy—excited—like it was a game or a puzzle, and not my life she was talking about. At that moment, I kind of resented her for it. It's funny how quickly respect can turn into resentment.

A few feet in front of where William and Haden sat outside of my cage, against the back wall, she stopped. "Hello, Haden."

He looked back down to his cards and started adjusting and shifting his hand. "Hey," was all he said, and he didn't even look up.

"Are you going to be here all night?"

"Yup. Straight through the moon cycle. Got babysitting duties." He slammed his cards down on the floor in front of him and yelled out, "Rummy! What's that, twenty-two games for me and three for you, is it?"

"Whatever," William said, as he gathered the cards into a pile and started shuffling. "I think your girlfriend wants to talk. Why don't you take it outside?"

If looks could kill, William would have dropped dead from Haden's glare. "She's not my—"

"It's cool," Amelia interrupted. "I'm sure we can catch up later. I need to go anyway. Bye." The door was already shutting behind her before anyone could react.

"Wow, rude much? What was that?" I asked.

Haden just shrugged. "What? I have a girlfriend. I don't need Amelia messing it up."

William scoffed under his breath. "Iris is not your girlfriend. Hell, she won't even go out with you."

"I'm working on it, OK."

"Wait, I don't get it. Iris is a weretiger. You're a werewolf," M said, leaning on the bars of his cage.

Haden just looked at him, "And your point?"

"Well, how would that even work? I mean it's like cats and dogs, they just don't... you know." Merick tried to explain.

"No, I don't know," Haden said.

They were going around and around, and I knew it could continue all night, so I decided to step in, "His point is that Amelia's a werewolf, like you. Even I can smell it on her. The two of you make perfect sense. Besides, Iris already told me that weretigers don't mate. They're independent. They don't even form packs like the werewolves do. You two are nothing alike." *Not to mention the fact that Remy is in love with her, and for years they've had plans to run away together, or something like that.* "Why waste your—?"

"It's the challenge," William said.

"What?" I asked.

"Oh," Merick said. "Now I get it. Dude, that's never gonna happen." He was trying hard, but having a hard time containing his laughter.

Oh that smile, I thought to myself, as William continued explaining. "Haden over here thinks he can tame Iris, get her to notice him, and then she'll fall in line like all the other women who seem to fall at his feet."

"That's not—" He stopped himself. I had a feeling he had thought better of lying.

"Yeah, good luck getting Iris to *fall in line,*" Merick said playfully. "From what I've seen, she's not really one for taking orders and doing what everyone else wants. She's too much of a...I don't know...a—"

"Hard ass?" William asked.

"I was going to say leader, but yeah, I guess," Merick said.

"What do you know anyway?" That was the end of the conversation, because Haden left.

I could see Merick out of the corner of my eye, just staring at me. "What?" I asked.

"So you like my smile huh?" he asked.

I could feel my cheeks turning red under his gaze, but I didn't turn away. *"You weren't supposed to hear that."*

"I like yours too."

Yup, I was definitely blushing.

35

I'm not sure when Haden came back because the lack of sleep was starting to hit me again. I was so tired and, with a full stomach after eating another plate of raw meat, I finally fell asleep.

"M?" I was jarred awake by screams, Merick's screams.

"He can't hear you now," Haden said, standing just outside Merick's cage and looking down at him. "The shift does something to your hearing. Makes things unrecognizable. At this point, all he knows is the pain."

I stared at Merick thinking back to my own change. The pain had been excruciating, but Haden was right, I remembered being relieved that I couldn't hear the sound of my own screams. "Interesting."

"What?"

Crap, did I say that out loud?

"Nothing, I was just thinking." I knelt down next to M's cage and called out to him, *"M, can you hear me?"*

Nothing.

"M, can you hear me? Growl if you can hear me."

Nothing.

Maybe if I were in animal form, I could— "Can lycanthropes communicate, in animal form I mean?" I asked, looking up at Haden.

"They can."

I turned to watch the others in their cages. "Even different breeds? Like wolves and lions or bears and tigers?"

He was watching me carefully. I could see him out of the corner of my eye, but even more—I could feel him. When I turned to him, our eyes met, and just for a second his eyes flashed from their natural dark brown to a golden yellow. "Yes," he answered.

"How?"

"You're just full of questions today, aren't you?"

I didn't answer.

"I can't explain how we can communicate, we just can. It's almost..."

I waited.

And waited.

"Telepathic?" I asked.

"Yeah, I guess so. I'm not sure if that's the right word, it's more—intuitively. It's more feelings and emotions than it is words, but yeah, I guess telepathically works."

Interesting.

"Hey, can I ask you something?"

"You just did," Haden said as he returned to his seat next to William.

"Ha-ha, you're so funny. Not."

He just rolled his eyes.

"So," I continued. "Is it hard for you, being cooped up in here with us during the moon cycle? Don't you want to shift too?"

"It's not like that for me. I've been a lycanthrope for so long now, the moon cycle doesn't really affect me anymore. I can shift whenever I want to."

I remembered what Iris had told me before, *"We can shift whenever we want, but we can only feed—hunt—during the three days of the moon cycle."*

"Yeah, but you're giving up your chance to hunt. I would have thought a guy like you would be—"

"I do what I'm told." I was certain he'd rather be out hunting, but something was keeping him here, something other than just Remy's instructions.

"I don't take orders," the werelion, Jabari, had said to me when I was outside the sector walls. I remembered how adamant he had been, how important his independence had been.

"Wolves, you're loyal, aren't you?"

"Only if you earn our loyalty."

I watched as M paced back and forth in his cage. His wolf eyes were foreign to me, and yet I still felt a pull to him, a connection. I knew he was loyal to me, but it was more than that. It was love. I so wanted to make him hear me—make him give me a sign that he was all right in there.

If I were in my wolf form, then maybe I could get through to him. It was worth a shot, but I wasn't so sure I could make it happen. *It can't hurt to try, right?*

36

Considering I had already destroyed one set of clothes during my first change, rather aggressively pulling them off and throwing them to the floor, I decided not to destroy the new clothes Amelia had brought me. That meant that this time, since I had already found myself naked in front of everyone who was here now, at least the ones who would remember, I decided to undress first.

I wrapped my thin blue blanket around me as I started to undress. It was awkward and uncomfortable, but at least it provided the idea of privacy. By the time my pants were nicely folded, and I was trying to pull my shirt over my head, all while holding onto the blanket, I could feel Haden and William secretly watching me from over their cards. "You know, it's not really polite to stare," I said.

William cleared his throat and quickly looked away, "You're right. I'm sorry."

"Whatever. What are you doing anyway?" Haden asked.

Is it really so odd that I'm undressing before I shift?

"Well, I don't really have an endless supply of clothing, so instead of ruining this set even more, I'm taking them off before I shift."

"Before you shift? You mean you can feel a change coming on?" Haden had put his cards down and was standing gripping the bars of my cage like he was waiting for a show to start.

"No, not exactly," I said.

"So what's the plan? You're just going to hang around naked on the off chance that you *might* shift?"

"Well, seeing as you two get to see me and all the others naked throughout this whole process, I guess I just need to embrace it. I mean, they all get the luxury of not remembering, but not me. Right? I get all the wonderful memories." I stood there staring right back at him. I wasn't going to let him shake me.

"Leave her alone, perv," William said. Haden did as he was told, or at least he sat back down—he didn't stop watching. I could feel his eyes on me.

"Somehow I shifted back…early, right?" I said.

"Yeah."

"I'm both vampire and lycanthrope, right?"

"Yeah."

"So, to say that I'm different wouldn't really be a stretch, right?"

"Yeah, no, you're different all right."

"Then, what makes you think I can't just shift whenever I want?"

At this point I was standing there, in only my panties and the thin blue blanket, but it wasn't what I looked like that got their attention; it was what I had said. Both William and Haden, as if choreographed, put down their cards, stood up, and crossed, step-by-step, slowly, to my cage. "Can you?" they asked at the same time.

"I guess we'll see." I slid my panties to the floor, from under the blanket, and stepped out of them.

I can do this. I can do this. It was like a mantra playing over and over in my mind.

Then, Remy's voice interrupted my thoughts, *"If you do decide to shift again this moon cycle, maybe try for a lion this time."*

I wondered if I actually could do it. *I can do this. I can do this. I can do this.*

I knelt down.

"You have no idea what you're doing do you?" Haden teased.

"Shut up." I tried to ignore him, but he just continued.

"Why are you kneeling?"

"Why are you talking?"

"It's not like there's a process. You don't have to get into position, be on all fours, and howl at the moon," he said.

"Then what?" I hadn't even realized I had stood up, dropping the blanket to the floor, before I was gripping his hands over the bars and standing nose to nose with him. "If you're such an expert then you tell me. What is it that triggers your wolf?"

He tried to pull away, but I was holding too tightly and he couldn't move. "It's a…a feeling—a need. Almost like…" He was breathing faster, and I could feel the weight of his eyes on my naked body. "…it's like my beast wants to break free."

"Your beast?"

Hmm. He sounds like Iris.

"Yes, my beast." His voice came out in a low rumble. "I can feel him, running—pushing at my skin—trying to escape." His eyes were closed now and his hands, held in place by mine, gripped the bars of my cage so tightly that I thought he just might pull them free.

"What do you do?"

"Nothing. I don't stop him. I just give in to it and let it happen."

I stepped back, letting go of his hands, and he quickly backed away. "Just give in to him?"

"Yeah."

I closed my eyes and focused on the beasts within me. For weeks, they had been there, eager to escape, and I knew they were still there even if I couldn't feel them. *Where are you?* I asked.

What I felt next, was the strangest thing I've ever experienced. I could feel the excitement of my wolf growing by the second. She could smell Merick, and I could tell she wanted to get to him, but she didn't rush forward. Not like I expected. She hung out somewhere deep inside. My lion, however, came right to the surface. She brushed up against me, and I could feel my chest rumble as she let out a steady yet soft roar. It felt like a warm hug and a deep tissue massage all at the same time.

"You smell like..."

I opened my eyes, and William was sniffing the air around him.

Haden followed suit. "She smells like...like lion." Our eyes met and I couldn't help but smile. "Just let go, give in to it. She'll know what to do," he said.

Give in to my beast. It seemed to make sense.

I closed my eyes again and whispered, "Come out."

Nothing.

"Come out."

Nothing.

"COME OUT!"

In a burst of sticky gooey slime I found myself standing on all fours looking up at the shocked faces of William and Haden, who had both stepped back from my cage in order to avoid the goo explosion.

It hadn't worked. They were covered.

I moved around the cage, turning my neck, stretching my legs, rubbing my paws along the rough floor, getting used to the feel of my new form. I shook my body, flinging the goo around my cage and off of my fur. I felt different this time. The transformation hadn't been as painful. Maybe because it happened all at once. Maybe because I knew what to expect. I'm not really sure. I just knew it was different than before.

My sense of smell was heightened. Merick's clean, fresh scent washed over me like a wave. There was a bitterness in the air too, something I hadn't noticed before, an unpleasant smell coming from— William. *Vampire blood?* I wondered.

"What is she doing now?" William asked as I sniffed the air in their direction.

"Ha, she's picked up your scent," Haden said as I stepped closer, reaching my front leg through the bars.

I felt stronger—fiercer. I felt like I could claw my way out of the cage if I wanted to. *Do I want to?* I wondered. *No, I don't think I do.*

It wasn't that I liked my cage, because I didn't. Being confined didn't feel right. However, there was a burning hunger in the pit of my stomach that desperately needed to be calmed. Logically, I knew that if I made it out of the cage I would do something I, the human me, would regret.

I guess that's why they cage the new lycanthropes in the first place, I thought. *Hmmm, I don't think I'm supposed to be thinking logically right now.* Just another advantage I seem to have over the other new lycanthropes.

I paced on the side of the cage I shared with M. He had stopped moving. He was lying on the floor of his cage, staring straight at me, with his chin on the floor and his paws straight out.

A low, guttural howl made its way from deep in his chest as he crawled his way, submissively, on his belly, toward the bars of my cage. He was worried about me. I wasn't sure how I knew, but I knew.

Haden was right, it isn't telepathy—it's different. Merick wasn't communicating words, but I knew exactly what he was thinking—feeling.

When I scanned the rest of the room, I could see Hudson fighting against the bars of his cage, trying to get out. Trying to get to me. A loud thunderous roar came from deep in his chest— longing? Maybe, or maybe a warning to Merick because, in response, Merick turned toward Hudson and growled back a long, deep, husky response. They stood there staring across the room in a standoff.

Men, I thought, shaking my head and backing away.

The door burst open. "When…? How, how did it happen?" Amelia asked as she rushed to my cage.

"How did you—?" Haden and William started.

She pointed to the ceiling above them. "Camera. I just got the call, but when? How?"

"Five minutes ago, maybe," William answered. "She got undressed and then just shifted."

"Just like that? That's fantastic." She was kneeling down at the side of my cage fumbling in her medical bag. "I need to get a blood sample. If I get her close to the bars do you think you can hold her down?"

37

I could have just let her do it. I knew she needed the blood sample, and I honestly had nothing against her taking it. But that didn't stop me from backing away when she tried. I guess, even as a massive werelion, I'm still afraid of needles.

"Come here kitty, come on," Amelia called out, as she held out a handful of raw meat through the bars of my cage.

How insulting, I thought. *I'm not a kitten, I'm a lion. I'm not going to fall for that.*

Then I did.

The meat smelled so good that I couldn't help myself. I made my way across the cage and took it right out of her hand.

She let me.

I knew it was a trap and yet, I didn't care.

It was my own fault when William slipped his arms around my neck and flipped me onto my side. I struggled, but, being a vampire, he was incredibly strong.

I was distracted when Haden made his way into my cage and climbed on top of me to hold my body flat against the floor so that Amelia could get a better angle on the vein in my front leg. As soon as I felt the sting of the needle I started struggling against him.

"Hurry up, will ya? I'm not sure how long William can hold her down, and I really don't want to be in here if she does get free," Haden said.

No, you don't, I thought.

"Afraid of a little shifter, huh?" Amelia asked, and I could tell she was just goading him, but I didn't like being called a little shifter.

I was just about to whip my head around and yank the needle out with my teeth when I saw Merick, in full wolf form, standing on his hind legs, pushing his body against the bars. At first I thought it was just my eyes playing tricks on me, but then I realized what was actually happening. His front paws shifted to human form, wrapped around the bars of the cage, and pulled the bars apart.

Wow.

"Leave her alone," he said through a human mouth that looked entirely out of place on his wolf form. As soon as the bars were far enough apart he leaped through, back in full wolf form, and lunged at Haden—who quickly let me go.

I felt the sting of another needle as Amelia pushed it into my back leg this time.

A loud, thunderous roar made its way up through my chest as I watched Merick bite down on the inside of Haden's throat. His teeth sliced through Haden's skin like butter, and the scent of blood filled the air all around me. I felt William's arms release me and heard the gate to my cage crashing against itself as he rushed inside.

William threw me across the cage, and Haden, now also in full wolf form, was leaping forward toward Merick. In their vicious struggle, Haden had already managed to claw open the inside of Merick's abdomen. I could smell the warm, fresh blood running down his body and dripping onto the floor. My vampire blood lust pushed my lion aside, and before I thought about what that might mean I was back in human form, naked, and fighting the urge to lick Merick's blood from the floor of the cage.

Amelia screamed from outside the cage as she jumped back, pulling the gate closed. "I, I didn't get the sample."

Merick was stumbling, trying to regain his balance, as he put himself between me and Haden.

'Don't do this M. You don't need to fight them for me. They aren't going to hurt me.'

He responded with a loud, painful howl, but he backed off, giving Haden and William the room they needed to get out of the cage and lock the gate behind them.

Once they were out, he fell to the floor, shifting back into his human form, and I was able to see the extent of his wounds. I pulled him to the corner, pressing my weight against the gash in his side. He just smiled up at me. "I'm fine. Don't worry, I'm fine." Then he pulled me down to the floor with him, wrapping his arms around me.

"You OK, Haden?" Amelia asked.

"Yeah, I'm cool." At the sound of his voice I turned. His neck, where Merick had bitten him, was fully healed.

"You want me to take a look at it?"

He just shook his head, watching her. There was a softness in his eyes that I hadn't seen before.

"What?"

"Nothing."

"Why are you looking at me like that?"

She noticed it too.

"You just..." Haden took two steps in her direction, and she backed into the bars of the cage across from mine. "You screamed."

"I...no I didn't."

"You were scared," Haden said, but he wasn't being mean. He wasn't teasing her like I would have expected.

"I wasn't scared. I was just frustrated, not being able to get the blood samp—"

"It was nice. I just mean, seeing your vulnerable side." He took another step toward her, closing the space between them. "You're always so reserved. It's nice to know that you aren't always in control."

They stood there, watching each other for what felt like a lifetime, and I was lost in the show. The feel of Merick's body against mine, as he curled up next to me brought me back to reality, and I drifted off, with the smell of him all around me.

"Get some rest, OK," she instructed Haden, before she turned to leave. "William, make sure he listens, please." The door shut softly behind her, and the room went silent.

38

When I woke up, Merick was gone. His scent still lingered, but he was nowhere to be found. His cage was empty, save for the thin blanket and flat pillow that still lay crumpled in a pile on the floor.

"Where is he?" I asked.

"Good afternoon to you too, sunshine," Haden said.

"Afternoon? What time is it?"

"Just after two o'clock. I was starting to think you'd never wake up." I glanced down at my monitor, Haden was right, it was just after two o'clock.

How had I slept so long?

I was standing now, stretching, while trying to keep the thin blue blanket around me. My muscles ached, and the pressure in my head was making me dizzy. I went over to the bars that separated Merick's cage from mine. They had been completely spread apart. "Where is Merick?"

Haden and William exchanged looks, but neither of them answered.

Gripping the bars, I stepped through, into Merick's cage. *How?* I wondered. How had he been able to manage a partial shift during his first moon cycle as if it were a conscious decision?

260

I turned back. "Where is he?" I asked again, but this time putting the full weight of my growing anger into the question.

"Amelia had him taken to the clinic. He wasn't healing like he should have. She needed to run some tests to find out what was wrong," Haden said.

What was wrong? I was pacing back and forth in Merick's cage. Lycanthropes are supposed to be able to heal just about any wound while in their animal form. It's one of their superpowers, like their inhuman speed and strength—the kind of strength Merick must have used to bend the bars of his cage. But then I remembered—Merick had shifted back. Maybe he hadn't given himself time to heal before shifting back to his human form.

I ran my hands up and down the misshapen bars wondering if I could do the same. Wondering if, looking back, Merick would do it all over again.

Why didn't he heal?

They were standing now, watching me closely—carefully.

"Why didn't he heal?"

"She's not sure."

"I need to see him." Haden opened his mouth to object. "Please," I added for good measure.

"Weren't you listening, he's been taken to the clinic. You can't see him because it wouldn't be safe for you. He's dangerous."

"He isn't dangerous. He would never hurt me. He was trying to protect me when..." The image of Haden's wolf lunging through the air at Merick came back to me. "When you attacked him. You're the one who should be locked up, not him."

I was getting angrier by the second. Clutching the bars I could almost feel the blood pumping through my veins. My skin began to burn, stretching in ways still so foreign to me. "No," I shouted, knowing what would come next. "No. I'm not gonna shift." I wasn't sure if I was trying to convince myself or command my beasts to stop. Either way it wasn't working.

"Maybe it'd be better if you did shift," William said. "You could let out some of that steam. You'll feel better."

"Shut up," I snapped at him. I knew he was only trying to be helpful, but I didn't need *helpful* right then. I needed out of that cage!

Gripping the bars I focused all of my energy there, into my hands. "I. Will. Not. Shift." I pulled until the creaking of the metal spreading apart stopped me. The hole was big enough for me to squeeze through, but William and Haden stood blocking my way.

"You really think that's a good idea?" Haden asked.

"No, but I need to see him."

"Wait just one more night," William said, as he stepped closer to the cage. "By the time you wake up tomorrow morning the moon cycle will be over, and you can go straight to the clinic and find out what's going on."

"That's enough." Ash's voice cut through the tension like a knife. I whipped around, and he was standing right behind me, in the cage. Before I knew it, his arms were around me and I couldn't move. "The boy is fine. He's being examined and will be released after the moon cycle, once he has fully healed. Until then, he will remain in the clinic under observation. You will continue to be here, until tomorrow. Do you understand?"

"Yes, sir."

"Good. Now sleep," Ash said, just before I felt a stinging pain shoot through my neck, and the room around me faded away.

39

My head was pounding when I woke up this time. "I'm getting sick and tired of—" My voice was scratchy and my throat burned, but that wasn't what stopped me. I looked around, and I wasn't in my cage anymore.

I was lying in a real bed with clean white linens and a soft fluffy pillow. There was a needle in my right arm, connected to a tube and a bag of clear liquid hanging on a pole at the side of my bed. Other wires were attached to my chest with small round stickers, leading to a monitor that beeped non-stop.

The room was small but quaint. The walls were white. On the wall to my right was a row of upper and lower cabinets, with a sink in the middle. To the left of the cabinets was a door, the only door in the room. On the wall that my bed faced was a dresser, covered in vases full of flowers. To my left was another wall, white like the others. There were no windows looking outside, but there was a painting of a small wooden cabin surrounded by trees and wildflowers. It was beautiful, and somehow familiar.

Am I at the clinic? I hadn't been to the sector clinic since I was a young child, but I didn't remember it looking like this. *If I'm in the clinic, then Merick must be close by.*

I sat up and started to untangle myself from all the tubes and cords I was connected to when I heard someone crying on the other side of the door.

The rhythmic sounds of feet slapping the floor as people made their way up and down the hall filled the air, but the soft crying seemed somehow clearer.

Knock. Knock. Knock.

I didn't move.

Knock. Knock. Knock. It came again.

"Why do you even knock? She never answers," Her voice was scratchy, broken, almost angry, as it came out between crying breaths.

I quickly lay back in the bed. *I never answer?*

"Can I come in?" someone called from the other side of the door.

"Yes." I called back so softly I was sure they hadn't heard, and surprised that my own voice sounded foreign in my ears—scratchy and painful. I didn't know who or what was about to come through the door when it opened.

The door opened without a sound and in stepped Amelia, wearing a long white lab coat over a black skirt and red button-down blouse. *Why is she dressed like that?* I wondered, only for a second, because the next thing I knew she was rushing to the side of my bed, screaming back over her shoulder.

"She's awake—she's awake. Get the doctor in here." She was grabbing at a cord on the side of my bed, attached to some sort of remote and pushing a large red button over and over.

"The doctor? I thought you were my doctor."

"Me? No, I'm not a doctor, not yet," she said. She was smiling, biting back what looked like laughter. "I can't believe you're awake."

"Did you say she's…?"

I leaned to my left, to see around Amelia. A woman with long red hair and the saddest blue eyes I had ever seen had just walked through the door. When our eyes met she started crying, but this time they were tears of joy, for a reason I didn't yet know. Her smile lit up her face as she ran to the side of my bed and pulled me into her arms. "How? Why? When? What happened? Is she…? Will she…? Can you talk? How are you feeling?"

My heart pounded in my chest. I was feeling crowded, and she was firing too many questions at me all at once. I tried to pull away, but she wouldn't let go. "Please… I need space."

She pulled back, reluctantly letting go. "I'm sorry, I just… I'm sorry." She sat down in a chair, pulling it as close to the side of my bed as possible, and held my hand. At least she wasn't smothering me anymore.

I watched her staring back at me, and there was a nagging feeling in my gut. I knew this woman from somewhere, but I couldn't pinpoint where. The longer I stared at her the more details I noticed. There were old scars on her arms and neck; *from where the vampires had fed on her,* I thought.

"Are you my… my donor?" I asked, wondering if they had sent her to me to feed on.

"Your donor?" she asked, shaking her head. "I don't understand."

"Did they send you to feed me?" My throat hurt, burned. It was making it hard to concentrate.

"Are you hungry? I can send for something if you'd like." I just shook my head. I *was* hungry, starving really, but I didn't feel like feeding just then.

She sat there, gripping my hand so tightly I thought she might rip it off. "Are you feeling all right? Do you want me to call in the doctor or one of the nurses?"

Her questions made no sense, seeing as ever since Amelia had come in the nurses and doctors had been rushing in and out of the room non-stop, talking among themselves, and checking all the beeping machines that surrounded me. Yet, they seemed so far away, almost like they weren't there with us in that moment.

"No, I'm all right. Besides, I think they've got things covered," I said, nodding at the two nurses whispering at the end of my bed. Her eyes seemed to stare right through me, into my soul. "Have...have you seen M?"

"M?" she asked.

"Merick."

"Merick is fine. I told you that earlier. They said you could hear me. I didn't think you could. You couldn't could you?"

Earlier? No. No, I don't remember.

"I...no, I—"

"Shhh," she said as she continued to smooth back my hair. "Don't worry. It will all come back in time."

"But I—" I wanted to tell her I had no idea who she was, why I was there, or even where I was, but her words stopped me.

"Don't give up. You have to fight this. You have to keep fighting," she said. "I won't give up on you."

Her words were so familiar. *Where have I heard—?* Then it hit me. The woman in the vision Micah had shown me, right before I killed him. The same woman I had seen lying on a table, surrounded by feeding vampires, the first time I had gone to the dining hall with Britt.

"Your breeder, she was special. Even she knew you would be the first-born." Amelia's voice played in my head. *"You are actually her only born who didn't get the fiery red hair."*

"Fiery red hair," I said to myself as I reached up, touching the hair that fell over her shoulder.

"The vampires turned her."

I wanted to ask, but I couldn't. I was lying there, holding her hair in my hands, and she was everything Amelia had said. She was my breeder. No one ever gets to meet their breeder, but mine was there. Right there. "You're my...my...?"

She smiled. "I'm your mom."

An alarm sounded from somewhere in the building, and I gasped for air as I jumped up, dropping my thin blue blanket to the floor at my feet. The cages around me were empty—even William and Haden were gone.

"Hello. Hello?" I called, but no one answered except for the echoing of my own voice bouncing off the walls around me.

Alone. Again.

The End for Now

Keep read for an exciting preview of

SECTOR C
THE BRIDGE

The final installment of

The SECTOR C Series
By Nina Soden

http://www.ninasoden.wordpress.com
http://www.twitter.com/Nina_Soden

1

I have always been taught that every being has a purpose, and I believe this to be true. In Sector C, where I grew up, life is organized and efficient, and although it is not completely predictable, it is intentional. Every meal is scheduled, every birth is preordained, every task is monitored, and every relationship must be approved by the High Council. I was taught from earliest childhood that life in Sector C was a gift. I was taught that I was fortunate to be allowed to fulfill my purpose in Sector C, whatever that purpose proved to be. In Sector C, I was safe, cared for, and...as I would soon find out...asleep.

When I woke up in the holding cell, I knew instantly that something was different, although I couldn't pinpoint exactly what it was. It would take time for me to be fully awake, but the change had already begun. My eyes had been opened to understanding the possibilities. Although I didn't know it at the time, I would soon realize how I had been deceived. We had all been deceived into believing that the powers that be, those who ran Sector C, had our best interests at heart and protected us from the evils that roamed freely in the wastelands beyond the sector walls.

It was not a comforting realization, knowing that things were changing yet not understanding how, but it was one I now knew I had to accept—and deal with.

I woke up to the thought that the "monsters" outside in the wastelands—the humans—the discarded and desperate ones, the angry ones, and the deserters who had fled of their own accord, were just that—humans—and not truly monsters. The fears of the generations who came before me had kept me caged. Fear had kept us all caged, in slumber. Although, that didn't mean real monsters didn't exist. They just weren't who I thought they were.

There were so many unanswered questions that had plagued me since Selection Week, and now they had solidified into one clear "need to know": Why? Why had I been injected with not one but two viruses that changed my genetic makeup? I had heard the lies: all about how I was to be the mother of a hybrid race that would bring peace to the lycanthropes and vampires. But that wasn't how they treated me. They treated me like some kind of guilty secret, not a redeemer or a liberator. That one clear question challenged everything I had ever been taught. It was the question we had been taught never to ask: Why? To what *purpose*? And yet, I had begun to question everything. I was finally ready to find the answers. I was finally ready to wake up.

Also by Nina Soden

The Blood Angel Series

What if everything you thought you knew about yourself and the world turned out to be wrong? The Blood Angel Series is set in a world very much like our own, yet Atlanta isn't just an ordinary city and Alee Moyer isn't just an ordinary girl. Having barely survived her childhood it will take the death of her father for the truth of her bloodline to come out. Even if it means losing her identity or even her life, she won't be able to escape her true destiny as the first surviving dhampir in history. Surrounded by a new world where the horror films she grew up watching have become reality and the most unlikely characters have become her lifeline, Alee must find herself and her purpose if she hopes to survive.

http://www.ninasoden.wordpress.com
http://www.twitter.com/Nina_Soden
https://www.amazon.com/author/ninasoden

www.ingramcontent.com/pod-product-compliance
Lightning Source LLC
Chambersburg PA
CBHW050015180626
46810CB00002B/429